# PROPERTY OF CHAOS KEEPERS MC

## WHY CHOOSE MC ROMANCE

### T.O. SMITH

Formatting: Tiff Writes Romance

Cover Design: Tiff Writes Romance

Editing: Tiff Writes Romance

Proofreading: Kimberly Peterson

*For Riley, my reason for everything that I do.*

*For every reader who loves a lot of fucking with little plot... and sword crossing. There's lots of sword crossing.*

## NOTE FROM THE AUTHOR:

This book contains elements and situations that some readers may not find enjoyable. These include elements of BDSM, more sex than plot, torture, graphic violence, murder, blood spill, group sex, anal sex, and gun violence.

If any of the above is triggering for you, I advise against reading.

If you have any questions before reading, please reach out to me via email (authortosmith@ gmail.com), Instagram, or Facebook.

Happy reading!

# CHAPTER 1

*Capone*

I f there was one thing I loved in this world, it was fucking one of my men, and when there were five of them to sink my cock into... It was like being submerged into Heaven on Earth.

There would be six, but Smokey wasn't interested in sex, which was fine. I loved him regardless of his lack of sex drive. He got my affection in other ways.

With five men to fuck *plus* a woman, one might think I'd get my fill, but nope. I was an insatiable beast.

And the only thing better than sinking into one of my men was sinking into our woman or watching her get railed by one of them. And fuck, if I thought *we* were insatiable? Our woman could take cock all day long and never get tired of it. The only reason she didn't was that we forced aftercare on her and made sure she took care of herself.

April watched over her shoulder with half-lidded eyes, her dark hair a fucking mess, as she watched River grip the sheets in his fists, grunting as I slid inside of his tight ass. River was slim with tattoos everywhere. But he was lethal as fuck if I needed him to be, and he loved getting fucked hard with complete abandon. He *wanted* it to hurt, to burn. And fuck, I loved being the one to inflict pain upon him.

"Shit. Shit. Shit," he hissed, his eyes no doubt rolling back in his head as I brushed against his prostate.

I leaned over him, my fingertips digging into his hips. "She's waiting," I rumbled in his ear before sucking his lobe into my mouth. I gripped his cock in my hand to the point it hurt, groaning when his ass clenched around me. Shit, it felt so damn good when he did that. "Don't leave our woman waiting, River. She's always such a good girl for us."

April whimpered at the praise, and I flashed her a soft smile. The rest of us were harsh and brutal with each other, but April? She was our soft spot— our weak link but also the one who made us strong. And we protected her and loved her like she was the most fragile thing in the fucking world. Because to us, she was.

"On your back," River gruffly told her. "Let us watch you while I fuck you raw."

I shivered, and I wasn't even the one he was talking to. Fuck, my boy had a way with words.

I dug my fingers into his hips, grunting as I slid out and pushed back into him, unable to help himself. He hissed a breath through his teeth, and we both watched as April flipped her curvy, soft, tattooed body onto her back, spreading her thighs for River, giving both of us a perfect view of her pretty, pink pussy.

"God, look at how wet she is," River growled, sliding his fingers between her folds, sliding her juices all over her, coating her in her own slickness. "How bad do you want me inside you, tat?"

She sank her teeth into her bottom lip at the sound of his special nickname for her falling off his lips. River was our tattoo artist, and the first time he'd tattooed her, he'd called her tat, and it stuck for them.

"So bad," she whispered. "It hurts, River. Make it stop hurting. I'm *aching*."

"*Godfuckingdammit*," I growled in one breath. I both loved and hated hearing her beg so fucking sweetly. Loved it because despite her acting like a whore most of the time, she was still so sweet and innocent when she begged. Hated it because it took every bit of my restraint not to spill inside River's tight ass. "Get inside of her so I can fuck you properly, boy," I snarled.

He leaned over her, bending his body, his hands planted on either side of her head. With my hand wrapped around his girth, I angled him into her pussy, groaning when I felt just how wet she was. Christ, I loved how much she wanted us. She was so unashamed of it, too, which just made it so much hotter. So much better.

And just to think, she once told us she wasn't sure if she could take all of us since she hardly ever got wet for her piece-of-shit ex.

Baby girl just hadn't been with real men before. Men that cared about her. Loved her. Worshipped her. Took care of her.

"Yes, yes, yes," April chanted, her ankles hooking around River's slim waist. I gripped those ankles in my hand, keeping her just like that as River fucked into her and I fucked into him. Their mouths found each other in a wet, messy kiss, their moans and groans fueling me as I wrecked River's tight hole.

Leaning over River's back, I slipped my tongue between their mouths, licking both of them. "Come," I snarled. "Now."

April cried out, shattering at my command, and River grunted, spilling into her hot, dripping pussy. He quickly pulled out of her, and I pulled out of him, watching as his cum began to roll out of her swollen pussy when he rolled to his back beside her.

"Not nice to let go of what he so eagerly gave you, baby girl," I teased, scooping his cum up to slip it back inside of her. She moaned, her eyelids fluttering. Then, I slid inside of her as well, licking a path up her neck. "You going to take my cum, too, baby girl? Be a regular old cum dumpster for me?"

"Yes," she whimpered, meeting me thrust for thrust, sweat making her hair cling to her face. "Give it to me." She reached up, her nails digging into my shoulders. "I want it so bad, Capone."

"*Gooood*, her mouth," River groaned, cupping his balls.

I reached over and gripped his cock. I knew it was tender, but my boy craved pain. He cursed and arched his back, his face screwed up in pain, but he didn't push my hand away. I jacked him off with my slick fingers as I fucked our woman into the mattress.

His cum splattered over my hand, and then I smeared it across April's face before leaning down to lick it off of her. She cried out, squirting all over me, and with a snarl of her name, I spilled my cum into her cunt.

"Such a good girl," I praised, licking my fingers clean of River's cum now that her face was clean. River leaned over and softly kissed her, rubbing his hand over her body to soothe her. Once she wasn't shaking and crying anymore from her orgasm, I gently scooped her worn-out body from the bed. "Aftercare, baby girl."

She linked her arms around my neck. "Bath?" she sleepily asked.

I pressed my lips to the top of her head. "For a little while. Then you and River can take a nap."

She pressed a kiss to my pulse in response. A shiver rolled down my spine.

Fuck, she had me wrapped around her pretty little finger.

River strolled past me into the bathroom, starting the water in the huge garden tub I had installed just for our woman. While I cradled her in my arms, River poured in her favorite lavender-scented bubble bath and Epsom salt. Using his hand, he swirled the water around before stepping into the tub and settling in. Then, he nodded once at me, letting me know he was ready to take her off my hands so I could get in with them without risking injury to her if I fell or slipped.

April allowed me to set her on her feet in the water. River clasped her round hips before easing her down between his thighs and pulling her back flush to his chest. I stepped into the tub after she was comfortable and settled with my back against the other end. April shut her eyes as I grabbed her right ankle. She moaned when I pressed my thumbs into the sole of her foot.

"That feels so good," she throatily groaned. My cock jerked, already coming awake, but I ignored it. She needed aftercare and rest now. Not more sex, no matter how much I wanted it. I had five other men to choose from if I really wanted to get off again.

Hawke would probably be down. He was as insatiable as I was, and while he was definitely a dom, he enjoyed submitting to me. I'd never forced it upon him; it was something he naturally did. And he loved having his boundaries pushed. He was the one I could get roughest with—and fuck, did I.

"What are you thinking about?" River asked, his foot nudging my inner thigh.

I glanced up at him as I settled April's foot on my thigh, reaching forward to grab her right ankle. Her eyes stayed closed as she relished in the feel of me relaxing all of her sore muscles. She spent a lot of time cleaning up after us and cooking for us, so I knew her feet needed a damn good massage. No better time to give it to her than during aftercare.

"Hawke," I rumbled.

April hummed. "I think he's with Brewer."

I chuckled. They'd be holed up for a while then. No doubt, Hawke was brutalizing every single one of Brewer's holes. The image that fired up in my mind had me groaning. Fuck, it was perfect. All of my men were beautiful together. Watching them was just as good as being with them.

A light knock sounded on the bathroom door. I turned my head, arching a brow at Tank. His dark hair was a slight mess on his head. His thick, muscular body was covered by a t-shirt and jeans, much to my distaste. He was my Vice President, and also the only man I would bottom with. And shit, did Tank know how to fuck. He had a way of making me lose my fucking mind when I was beneath him... or on him.

He walked over to the tub and crouched beside it, reaching out to run his fingertips over April's cheeks. Her lips were softly parted, and she was officially asleep, not even stirring at his gentle touch. "Heard her moaning and begging all the way downstairs," he told me. I smirked. I'd done my job as her man then. He cradled the back of River's head and pressed a kiss to our boy's swollen lips. "Heard you too, boy."

River smirked. "What can I say? Capone can fuck."

Tank arched a brow at him. "Don't be sassy, boy. Or I'll make sure you can't walk."

River's pupils blew out, and a shuddered breath ripped from his lungs. I chuckled and smoothed my hands up April's waxed legs, massaging her calf muscles. "Make sure you take a nap with April when you finish in here," Tank told River. Then, he turned to look at me, his eyes running over me. His eyes locked on my hard cock for a moment. He licked his lips before standing to his full height. "If you want to take care of that later, come find me," he told me.

I grunted in acknowledgment because I was pretty sure I'd choke on my tongue if I verbally responded to him. Not only was Tank the only man I would bottom with, but he was also the only man capable of making me lose my fucking mind and forget my words.

# CHAPTER 2

*Tank*

Capone stepped into my room in a pair of sweats, his shirt missing—not that I was complaining. The man was built beautifully with abs, a hard broad chest, and thick biceps. He had a body worthy of art; I would know since I enjoyed seeing River sketch him from memory.

I arched a brow at Capone and set aside the TV remote. He laid on the bed beside me, and I curled my arm around him before turning on my side to face him.

"You okay?" I rumbled.

He nodded. "Need a quiet place to rest for a minute," he mumbled, his eyes shutting. "River and April have taken over my bed." I knew he wasn't complaining; Capone loved those two to pieces.

I chuckled and squeezed him closer. I was bigger than Capone—almost twice his size—and I loved it. It meant I got to give him cuddles like this where he was dwarfed by my frame. He'd never admit it, but Capone liked it when I cuddled him.

"You can rest here whenever you want," I reminded him. I began to trace the ridges of his tattooed spine. "Sure you're okay?"

He yawned and nodded his head. "Just fucking tired."

I brushed my lips to his cheek. Capone had a lot resting on his shoulders. Not only was he the president, but he took care of all of us. And he struggled to lean on anyone enough to let them share in his burdens.

"You know, you could use some aftercare, too, babe."

Capone chuckled. "You are my aftercare."

I made a small rumble of pleasure that resonated from deep within my chest. "I'll be your aftercare whenever you want me to," I promised him. I brushed a kiss to his brow. "Get some rest. I'm going to finish this movie."

He nodded and burrowed his face against my chest, his body relaxing against mine as sleep took him under within a few mere seconds. He really had been tired.

I ran my eyes over his features as his face relaxed in sleep. I really wished he took better care of himself, but he was Capone. The president. The man we all turned to in our time of need. He had the weight of the world on his shoulders, and he wasn't good at sharing that burden. Not even with me—his VP and his equal.

So, I did things like this for him when I could. It was the only way I could take some of the burden from him, even if just for a moment.

Capone wasn't God, no matter how much he liked to pretend he was. He had needs, too. He was human, just like the rest of us.

All I could do was try to take care of him as well as he took care of the rest of us.

———

**TWO DAYS LATER**

I groaned and spread my thighs wider apart to accommodate Rider's slim body. We'd come in from a run late last night and crashed into bed together after a quick shower, too tired to do anything else. But apparently, Rider was well-rested because he was waking me up with some fucking *amazing* head.

Two days had passed since Capone had curled into bed with me, but he seemed to be doing a bit better since spending the night with me and letting me take care of him. It was the only reason I hadn't put up a fight when he'd sent me on the run with Rider yesterday morning to do the gun sale.

"That's it, boy," I rumbled, lacing my fingers in Rider's purple hair. He moaned around my cock, the ball of his tongue piercing sliding over my head just like I loved before he sucked me deep into the back of his throat. I moaned and tightened my fingers in his hair, thrusting even deeper down his warm, tight throat. Like the greedy whore he was, he only ground his cock against the mattress, seeking friction as he swallowed around me.

"Fuck," I rasped, the muscles in my thighs tightening when he continued to suck me even harder, his tongue licking all over me like he just wanted to steal all the flavor off of me he could. I yanked on his hair and popped him off of me. "Get up here. *Now*," I growled. Fuck, he had a way of driving me fucking insane. If he kept up with that wicked tongue, I wasn't going to last.

He grinned at me and licked his lips, flashing that fucking wicked tongue ring at me. His thighs straddled me, powerful with muscles, and he gripped my cock, rubbing the head along his hole. I closed my eyes, groaning when his slickness spread over me.

"Been playing with yourself this morning?" I rumbled, opening my eyes to look at him. His colorful tattoos were on display, his pierced nipples gleaming at me in the dim light of the room. The pierced tip of his cock glinted in the morning light, teasing me. Reaching out, I rubbed my thumb over the tip of his cock, gently pulling on the bar running through it. He hissed a breath through his teeth, his eyes momentarily rolling back in his head.

I loved using his piercings to tease him.

"Prepping," he rasped, shuddering when I thumbed the head of his cock again. Then, he seated himself on me, and I growled his name, my hands latching onto his thighs with a bruising grip.

He groaned and pressed his hands to my chest, his black-colored nails gripping the hair there. I hissed a breath through my teeth, but then the pain that shot through my chest was quickly forgotten when he began to ride me, his thighs tensing beneath my hands as he expertly bounced on my thick cock.

"That's it, boy," I praised. My neck muscles strained with the urge it took to not flip him over and fuck him into the mattress. "Ride that cock. You like how big it is? How much it stretches you?"

Rider whimpered and panted, nodding his head, his green eyes glazed over with lust. He gasped and choked when my cock brushed his prostate. His body shuddered, and I angled my hips for him, making sure I hit that sweet spot inside of him over and over until he was spurting cum all over my chest and stomach.

Flipping him onto his back, I hiked his legs up over my shoulders and pounded into his tight ass. He was moaning and whimpering like a perfect little whore, his muscles tightening as he took the pounding I was giving him.

"T-Tank," he choked. "*F-F-Fuuuuuuck,*" he cried out, his neck arching beautifully.

I leaned over him and molded our lips together, forcing my tongue into his mouth. He groaned and eagerly kissed me back, his tongue dancing with mine. With a snarl of his name, I spilled into his ass, marking him and dirtying him up.

"Shit," he whispered when I flopped to my back next to him. He closed his eyes and rolled on his side, snuggling against me. Rider was a hardass to the rest of the world, but with us—the club and April—he was soft as hell, and he was *extremely* touchy-feely. I loved how needy he could be. Couldn't get enough of it.

And we were his safe space. It meant the world to me that he trusted us enough to be his true self—crazy-colored hair, painted nails, and all. I'd never change him for the world.

"You good?" I asked him, running my fingers through his purple hair.

He nodded, pressing a kiss to my bicep. "Need a shower, but I don't think my legs will work."

I chuckled and brushed a kiss to the top of his head. "I'll help you bathe. Come on. I'm sure April will be up shortly making breakfast."

If anything made Rider get up, it was the idea of April, no matter what she might be doing. He rolled over and sat up. Slowly, he stood to his feet, his legs shaky. I quickly got out of bed and placed my hand on his lower back, walking with him to my shower.

Where I got the naughty boy off one more time just because I was a generous son of a bitch.

————

When we emerged from my room, Rider headed to his to get dressed, and I headed out into the main area. Sure enough, I could see April in the kitchen, working on breakfast for all of us. None of us had missed a meal since we took her in unless we were on the road. She took such good care of us. No one could ever replace her in our lives or in our hearts. She was a part of us.

Without her, we would surely crumble.

"Church, babe," Capone told me.

Nodding once at him, I held my finger up, signaling to give me a moment, and then I headed into the kitchen to greet our woman. She was wearing a pair of shorts that showed the curves of her ass cheeks and a soft crop top with no bra. If there was one thing April hated, it was wearing a bra. But honestly, I couldn't blame her. The contraptions looked uncomfortable. I couldn't imagine wearing one all the time.

"Good morning," I rumbled, wrapping my arms around her from behind and pressing a kiss to her cheek. Her belly was soft, and I couldn't resist rubbing my hands over the soft flesh.

"Hi," she said, turning her head to kiss me properly. I groaned and deepened it for a moment, but not long enough that she ended up accidentally burning herself or the food got ruined. I released her after and took a step back. If I didn't, I might end up setting her on the counter and fucking her into the middle of next week. To hell with the food.

"Sleep well?" I asked her, leaning on the counter next to where she was cooking.

She nodded. "Spent the night with River." River was the only non-officer member we had, and he'd gotten here shortly before April did. He'd been freshly released from prison with nowhere to go if he didn't want to return home, which was got him in trouble in the first place. He'd gotten caught up with the wrong people in exchange for somewhere to live, and they'd ratted him about the drugs in the house out to save their own asses.

So, when he showed up here needing a place to go, we took him in. It took Capone a minute to trust him, but River proved himself to us over and over. Now, Capone doted on him almost as much as he doted on April.

He was our sweet baby boy.

River stuck around here when we had to deal with club shit. He wasn't muscular by any means, but he could hold his own in a fight, and he was quick with his mind. And he was damn near perfection with a tattoo gun in his hand. Right here at home with April was where we needed him the most, and he didn't bat an eye when he was left behind with her. I was pretty sure he preferred to be with her anyway.

None of us thought he was bi at first, but then Rider caught him watching gay porn one day. Capone walked in on them fucking shortly after, and from there, he joined the rest of us.

There had never been jealousy among us. We shared with each other but didn't touch anyone outside of the club. It kept away drama with women, and it kept us safe. And we were all definitely satisfied.

And then April showed up, flipping everything out of sorts. Capone sent her away the first day she'd come begging for somewhere safe to stay with bruises discoloring her skin and tears streaming down her face. None of us had any idea why she thought we would protect her. We kept to ourselves for a reason, and we weren't friendly with anyone in town.

But then she came back the next day, barely conscious, covered in blood and more bruises, barefoot and shivering. Capone had been in town getting groceries for all of us when she popped up, and when she collapsed in my arms, falling unconscious, I'd taken the choice out of Capone's hands. I wasn't letting Capone toss her out a second time. I was terrified she would end up dead if we didn't take her in.

But the moment he'd seen her—battered and bloodied—Capone hadn't been able to turn her away again either. She'd been here ever since. It had taken mere hours for her to win over Capone once she was conscious, and I was pretty sure he was the most smitten with her out of all of us.

"Tank," Capone called from the entrance to the kitchen. I looked over my shoulder at him, arching a brow. "Church," he commanded, looking a bit impatient this time.

I rolled my eyes, kissed April one more time, and then slipped out of the kitchen, following Capone into the chapel. I took my seat on his left.

"What's on the table?" I asked, glancing at Capone since he'd been so fucking impatient.

"Got a run," he said. I grunted. Fuck, Rider and I had just gotten back from one. "I got the call about six this morning. Three crates for the Savage Crows."

"Grim or Copper?" Smokey, the road captain, asked, flicking his blonde strands out of his damn near black eyes. Smokey was... special. He had a sweet, tender soul, but I knew a monster lurked beneath his skin. He struggled with depression, and due to his past, he wasn't interested in sex in the slightest.

I was the closest to him. I'd been the one to rescue him and help him the most. And our bond had formed from that—a trauma bond. One that was damn near unbreakable.

PROPERTY OF CHAOS KEEPERS MC    23

"Copper," Capone told him. Smokey sighed. Everyone hated dealing with Copper. He was a fucking dick ninety-nine percent of the time, but no one wanted him as an enemy. So, we dealt.

"I'll plan the run," Smokey announced. "I'll let you and Tank know when I've got the details and who I want on the road with me."

Capone nodded once. "Good. Anyone else got anything to bring to the table?"

"Yeah—April," Brewer teased, making us all laugh. The number of times we'd laid that woman on this table and tag-teamed her was uncountable. My dick jumped behind my zipper at the thought of it. Fuck, she was always so beautiful when she was surrounded by all of us. Right where she belonged.

Capone shook his head and slammed his gavel on the table, adjourning church. We slipped out of the chapel just as April was plating up food and placing them on the table we always ate at. As soon as she was done serving everyone else and walking to the table with her plate of food, I dragged her onto my lap. She squeaked in surprise, and Capone caught her plate before she dropped it.

"Thank you, baby," I murmured, pressing a kiss to her cheek.

"Open," Capone ordered, holding up a forkful of eggs for her. She obediently opened her pretty mouth, allowing Capone to feed her.

"Ugh, it was my turn today," Hawke grumbled, playfully pouting at April.

We were all a little clingy with her. Couldn't help it. She was just so goddamn perfect.

April blushed. "First come, first serve," she teased, sticking her tongue out at him. I chuckled.

Hawke winked at her. "I'll remember that, doll."

I laughed when she sucked in a sharp breath, her pupils dilating at what that could mean.

So damn needy. I fucking loved it.

# CHAPTER 3

*April*

I squeaked in alarm when Capone suddenly lifted me from Tank's lap. I'd barely swallowed my last bite of food before he went all caveman on me. "Capone, what are you—hey!" I yelled when he tossed me over his shoulder. I groaned and slapped my palms to his ass cheeks in retaliation. He growled in warning, but if there was one thing I loved about bothering Capone, it was the punishments he delivered.

I called them funishments. The prez *knew* I was sometimes bratty with him on purpose. And he enjoyed doling out a little bit of pain when I needed—well really, wanted—it.

He smacked his hand on my ass, and a breathy moan spilled from my lips. Hawke winked at me as Capone walked past him.

"Enjoy, doll," Hawke rumbled, leaning back in his chair. He rubbed the pad of his thumb across his lower lip, and my breath hitched in my throat. Fuck, he had no right being that hot when he did that. Especially when his eyes darkened and he spread his legs a bit, letting me know what seeing me manhandled like this did to him.

"Stop teasing her," Capone growled, not even having to turn around to know Hawke was teasing me as he marched toward the stairs. I giggled, and Capone swatted my ass again, this time harder, making it sting. I hissed a breath through my teeth, dampening my panties at the same time. My eyes caught on Tank's, and he smirked at me.

"Goddammit, Capone," I growled, dropping my head so I was staring at his perfect, biteable ass. "That hurt."

He smacked my ass again, this time on the other cheek. I dug my nails into his back, groaning, letting my head fall the rest of the way, my dark hair curtaining my face and almost dragging the floor. "Watch your mouth with me, baby girl," he softly warned. I released my hold on his back, silently letting him know I was submitting. He hummed and rubbed my backside. My thighs clenched. "Good girl."

*Fuuuck.* I had a thing for being praised, and Capone fucking knew it. All of the men did, really. I liked a little bit of degradation too, but praise? Fuck— praise was my kryptonite.

I moaned. Capone kept me stabilized with his arm around the back of my thighs as he ascended the stairs, and finally, he made it to his room, which was the last one, all the way down the hall. I grunted when he suddenly tossed me over his shoulder and dropped me onto the mattress, my body bouncing when it hit the soft bed.

Gripping my ankles, he yanked my ass to the edge of the mattress before leaning over me, taking my lips in a slow, hot, drugging kiss. I arched into him, sighing into the kiss as I gripped his shoulders, dragging him down closer to me. Kissing him was like drowning in the ocean, waves knocking me in several directions, and suddenly being able to breathe again before tugged right back under. Completely at its mercy.

"I think you need a punishment for being bratty," he rumbled against my lips.

Opening my eyes, I licked the seam of his lips. He was already staring down at me, his dark eyes blazing with need. My breath caught in my throat. God, I couldn't get enough of how he always looked at me. Like he was the devil, and I was some combination of an angel and a demon wrapped up in a package he wanted to consume.

"What kind of punishment?" I asked him, my voice lowered so I wouldn't break whatever magic was happening between us. I slid my fingers into his dark hair, loving how soft the strands were as they sifted through my fingertips.

A wicked smirk tilted his lips all while he leaned more into my touch. Only a man like him could be soft and hard all at the same time. It was a bit addicting to experience. "The kind that makes certain little brats remember the rules before breaking them again," he rumbled. He cupped me between my thighs, and I whimpered, closing my eyes and spreading my legs further apart for him. "Like no orgasms."

My eyes snapped back open. "You wouldn't," I hissed. He'd *never* done that before. It would be too much.

He arched a brow at me. "I wouldn't?" he taunted. I swallowed thickly, realizing my mistake. I'd just *challenged* him. Oh, I was so fucked. So, so, so royally fucked. And *not* in the fun way that I wanted to be. "Just for that little bit, baby girl, you don't get to come until I tell you to. And maybe I won't let you come at all."

I shook my head and sat up. "Please, don't," I begged him. I gripped his cut in my fists, imploring him with my eyes to not do this to me. "I'll do anything, Capone." I hated being denied. He knew that. And this was the first time he was using it to his advantage. Suddenly, punishments didn't seem so fun anymore.

A cruel smirk twisted his lips. "Anything, baby girl?"

I didn't like the look of that smirk, but I nodded my head anyway. I couldn't handle being denied. Even now, I could feel my chest tightening from anxiety. The mere thought was freaking me the fuck out.

Capone's smirk widened, and he unbuckled his belt. "Good. Get on your knees on the floor," he commanded.

I quickly moved off the bed and lowered myself to my knees. While I was nervous to see what he was going to do in exchange for not punishing me like that, I knew he'd never do anything to harm me. All I had to do was let him know I didn't want this, and he'd stop. Capone was so damn good at reading my body language that words weren't even needed. It had happened before when I got overwhelmed.

*Hawke pressed the vibrator against my clit again. My legs shook. Tears streaked down my cheeks. I'd already had so many orgasms, I couldn't even count them anymore. My pussy was swollen and constantly dripping, and my ass hurt after experiencing anal for the first time, especially with how big Hawke's cock was.*

*"Hawke, please," I whimpered. A sob tore from my throat as another orgasm built. "I can't—please." Snot ran from my nostrils.*

*"You're doing so good for me, doll. So good. Such a perfect little fuck toy." He loomed over me, turning up the speed on the vibrator. I wailed. "You wanted this, remember? You begged me to treat you like a slut."*

*I shook my head, every muscle in my body locking up. I had asked him to do that, but I couldn't take it anymore. I really couldn't. "Hawke—"*

*"Stop," Capone suddenly commanded. He stood from where he'd been silently watching in a chair against the wall. Immediately, Hawke turned the vibrator off and began to unfasten the cuffs around my wrists and ankles. Capone slid onto the bed and pulled me into his arms, cradling me close.*

*"I thought—" Hawke rasped, pain flashing through his eyes. And guilt. So much guilt, it tore at my insides.*

*"Come here," Capone gently ordered. Hawke immediately settled against my back, and Capone wrapped him up in his arms with me. "She just wanted to be perfect for you, I think," Capone soothed him. "She didn't use the safeword you gave her. That doesn't fall on you, Hawke."*

*I sniffled. "I'm sorry," I cried. I did want to be perfect for him, and I thought safewording would ruin everything.*

*Capone brushed his lips to the top of my head. "Nothing to be sorry for, baby girl. You're still new to this. But your safeword is there for your safety. That could be physical, mental, or emotional. Use it. We'll never make you feel like shit for it. Never."*

*"Even I've safeworded," Hawke gently told me. I swiped at my cheeks. "It's nothing to be ashamed of, doll." He wound his arms around me, resting his chin on my shoulder. "What's your safeword?"*

*My chin wobbled. "Wolf," I whispered.*

*He pressed a tender kiss to my neck. "Good girl. Don't ever forget it."*

"Hands behind your back," Capone ordered, dragging me out of the memory, "and do not move them."

Swallowing thickly, I quickly linked my hands together behind my back. The move thrust my chest out, and he groaned as he lowered the zipper on his jeans. When he suddenly laid back on the bed, his booted feet planted flat on the floor, I frowned.

*What was he planning on doing?*

He pushed his jeans and boxers down before gripping his hard shaft, stroking it. My lips parted, and I clenched my thighs, heat rushing to my core. Swallowing thickly, I watched as he began to get himself off, my breathing quickening. Oh, this was *almost* as bad as being denied my orgasm. My mouth watered, eager for a taste of him that I knew I couldn't have.

I whined.

He turned his head, looking down at me. His cock looked so beautiful surrounded by his thick, tattooed, ring-covered fingers. One of his skulls glinted in the low lighting of his room. "You can come, baby girl, but only if you can make yourself come while kneeling on the floor with your hands behind your back."

My mouth dropped open. He couldn't be serious!

"If you don't come," he added, a wicked gleam burning in his dark eyes, "*no one* touches you until I get back from this run."

I shook my head, my heart racing in my chest. I craved all of these men, and Capone knew I craved sex mostly because I *needed* the physical intimacy that came with it. He wouldn't really deny me of that, would he?

One look into his eyes told me he most definitely would.

I swallowed thickly, my chest aching at the mere thought of not being able to be with my men like I wanted. "I hate you," I rasped.

He quickly stood from the bed and crouched in front of me. Gripping my chin with his fingers, his grip tight and a bit painful, he forced me to meet his eyes. "Don't be bratty because you suddenly don't like your punishment, April. You asked for this, remember?"

I sank my teeth into my lower lip, looking away from him. I choked when he suddenly forced my jaw open and shoved his fingers deep into the back of my throat. I moaned, my eyes sliding shut as I sucked on his thick digits, tasting him. My pussy clenched around absolutely nothing, desperate to have his cock inside of me.

He pulled his fingers from my mouth and then stood, shoving his dick into the back of my throat. I didn't have a gag reflex, so I swallowed around him, greedily sucking him, hoping that I could portray how sorry I was through a blow job. I didn't like being denied—not anything. Especially not my orgasms... and not his either.

"Such a good girl when you want to be," he rumbled, lacing his fingers in my hair. He pulled out of my mouth before gripping his cock and stroking it. "But you're still getting your punishment, baby girl." Tears welled in my eyes. He hummed, eyeing me with a primal look in his eyes.

Like he *wanted* to see me cry over his cock. "Depending on how good you are for me until I'm finished, *maybe* I'll let River come up here and get you off."

I whimpered but nodded. I watched him with hungry eyes as his hand quickened. He was so beautiful as he stroked his shaft, his fingers twisting and turning. And when he groaned, his head rolling back on his shoulders, I scooted forward and stuck out my tongue, looking up at him from beneath my lashes. The sound of my movement made him look down at me, and he growled my name before setting the tip of his cock on my tongue and shooting his cum down my throat.

He hadn't wasted it. And neither did I.

I swallowed it all down when he was finished, and he helped me to my feet before brushing my hair back from my shoulders. Then, he gripped my neck with both hands, dragging me closer to him. His nose brushed mine as he lowered his head. My heart raced in my chest. I loved how possessive his touch could be. I felt so safe like this.

"River will be reporting back to me while I'm gone, letting me know if you're a good girl or not, understand?" I quickly nodded my head. He brushed his lips over mine. "Go to River's room, baby girl. I'll let him know you deserve a reward."

I threw my arms around his neck, squeezing him tightly. "Please be careful," I pleaded. I hated it when he went on runs. I hated when *any* of my men had to leave home. Because they weren't guaranteed to come back in one piece... or alive.

He palmed my ass in his hands, squeezing tightly. His lips brushed across my temple, and I squeezed my eyes shut. "Always am, baby girl."

# CHAPTER 4

*Rider*

I watched as Capone shook hands with Copper, nodding his head a couple of times as Copper spoke. Capone gestured toward the weapons and said something before Copper inclined his head to him and stepped back.

I barely resisted curling my lip in distaste. God, I hated Copper. He was a damn good president. I'd give him that. But he was an asshole through and through. I hated it when our club had to deal with him, but it was easier to have him as an ally than an enemy.

Copper had power and his fingers in multiple pies. Being on his bad side wasn't something we wanted. So, while none of us liked him, we put up with him.

Capone strode over to me and crossed his arms over his chest as we watched Smokey handle the exchange. As the Secretary, Brewer handled the cash exchange, and I glanced over, making sure he was okay. As the Sergeant at Arms, I was supposed to protect Capone, but I protected all of them.

Losing one of them would kill a piece of me. If Capone would've allowed it, I would've created an officer title called Club Protector. But alas, he wouldn't. He liked the structure how it was.

Capone wasn't a fan of change.

"We need to get River out on these runs more," Capone quietly told me.

I shook my head in disagreement, immediately disliking that idea. And I knew the other guys would agree with me. "River is right where he needs to be—at home with April." While he was a patched member of the club, we all fiercely protected him—just about as much as we protected April. Though River had strength and I knew deep down he could handle his own, the thought of bringing him out here into the wild with the rest of us, where he could be hurt or killed, made me sick to my stomach.

It was just about equivalent to how I felt about bringing April on a run. It wasn't happening. River was our baby boy. He needed to be right at home where he was currently.

"He's a patched member, Rider," Capone murmured, keeping his voice low so our conversation wouldn't carry to any members of the Savage Crows MC's Mother Charter.

I shook my head, clenching my jaw. I was holding firm on this. "If you call a vote on it, I *will* vote against it," I warned him, looking at him out of the corner of my eye. He sighed, still watching what was going on around us. I focused on Smokey, watching the way the muscles in his arms flexed as he helped one of the SCMC members load the crates of weapons into the van. "River needs to stay at home with April. He's safe there, and he's good protection for our woman if something goes south while we're gone."

Capone grunted but nodded, relenting and putting an end to the conversation. I relaxed a little now that the wild-haired idea was out of his head, watching as the other crew got in their vehicles and drove off. We waited until we could no longer hear their engines driving down the road before we got on our bikes to head the other way back home.

"Time to get home," Tank said with finality as he swung his huge body over his bike. I licked my lips at the sight of him. Fuck, Tank made straddling a bike fucking erotic. "I believe we've got a hot as hell woman and fine ass man waiting on us."

Brewer winked at him. "Don't forget about us, babe."

Tank barked out a laugh and strapped his helmet to his head. "First one through the doors of the club-house is the first one that gets to have April."

No one sure as hell had to tell me twice. I slung my leg over my bike, gunned my engine, and tore off down the road.

I had a woman to get home to.

———

I rushed to the front door, shoving Brewer out of the way with a laugh. He hit the doorframe with an "Oomph," and I rushed through the door, cackling the entire way. April looked up from where she was chopping vegetables, an alarmed look on her face. Relaxing when she realized it was just me, she beamed, setting down her knife. "Rider!" she exclaimed.

Lowering my body, I pushed my shoulder against her abdomen and lifted her over my shoulder, being gentle with her despite handling her like a sack of potatoes. She shrieked in alarm, her hands gripping my belt. "What the hell, Rider?!" she yelled.

Brewer flipped me the middle finger. "You're a douchebag, babe."

I winked at him. "Remember that when I sink in your ass later to punish you."

He shivered, his eyes darkening a shade with lust. Some of us were more submissive than others, and Brewer was one of those submissives. He loved bottoming, and he had a thing for us telling him what to do. I wasn't much of a dom, but I did enjoy topping every once in a while. And topping Brewer's muscular, thick body was a surreal experience.

I chuckled and continued down the hall to my apartment. Once I kicked the door shut behind me, I dropped April onto the bed and pushed my cut off my shoulders, tossing it onto the end of the bed. April shivered in anticipation and gripped the hem of her shirt, tugging it over her head. I watched as she undressed while I pulled my own clothes off, and as soon as she was naked, I slipped my fingers between her thighs.

She was slick as hell. Always so damn ready. I never got used to it.

"Already wet, my girl?" I rumbled. Her tatted thighs trembled as I stroked her again.

Such a beautiful, needy girl.

Her cheeks turned a light shade of pink. "River just got done with me a little while ago."

Of fucking course, he did. The two of them were needy as hell, especially when they were alone and trying not to worry about us being on the road.

I groaned and dropped to my knees between her parted thighs, licking at her cunt to savor the taste of River's cum mixed with the essence of her. She cried out in shock, her fingers tangling in my purple hair. I let her ride my face and take what she needed. Sucking at her clit, licking into her swollen cunt—fuck, I couldn't get enough of the taste of them together.

Right before she came, I rose above her, and she whined, shaking her head, not wanting me to stop.

But then, I sank inside of her. Her eyes rolled back in her head, and her back arched off the bed. A shattered scream ripped from her lungs as she squeezed around me. I growled and gripped her thighs, pulling them up so her ankles hooked over my shoulders. Then, I pounded inside of her, fucking her and screwing her into the mattress.

"You're about to have a very busy day," I rasped, leaning over her with the backs of her knees draped over my elbows. She gasped at the new angle. Clinging to my sides, she took the battering I was giving her sweet core. "One of these days, my girl, two of us are going to get inside this sweet pussy at the same time. Fucking *wreck* you. Would you like that?"

"Yes," she cried, her body trembling. I growled, and just as she began to come again, she cried out my name. Surprising the fuck out of me, the door suddenly opened, revealing Tank. He was already naked, his hard shaft hanging heavy between his thick thighs. I groaned, running my eyes over him, my fists curling into the sheets so I wouldn't shatter before I was ready.

It took great effort to rip my eyes away from the beast of a man as he strode further into the room. Gripping April's chin, I forced my tongue in her mouth, stealing her remaining breath. "His turn, my girl," I murmured, pushing her face to the side so she could see Tank's massive frame standing here, his dick already wet with a little bit of lube and standing at attention. I winked at him. "Who'd you get inside?"

He hummed. "Capone." I groaned. I loved watching the two of those alpha males together. The only people they bottomed with were each other, and it was a goddamn sinfully beautiful thing to watch. "Move. It's my turn." When I pulled out of her, he pointed to the bed. "Let her clean you up."

Fuck, I hadn't even gotten to come yet. But if there was one thing I knew about Tank, he'd make sure I did before this was over.

As soon as I slid out of her and was out of the way, he flipped her over onto her belly and dragged her to the edge of the bed, her feet planted on the floor. She trembled in anticipation, her eyes hazy as they met mine. Fuck, she was so beautiful like this.

"You ready for me?" Tank asked her, running his rough palm down her spine. A full-body shiver rolled through her, her pupils blown and taking over her irises.

Heaving in tired breaths, she nodded her head, her fists clenching the sheets. She'd be sore after Tank got done with her, no doubt, but she wouldn't be able to voice any complaints while he was fucking her.

Not with my dick down her tight, wet throat.

# CHAPTER 5

*Tank*

I was already hard from Capone not letting me cum, ordering me to instead feed it all to April. God, the way that man still controlled me even when I was balls deep inside his tight ass... It was fucking unreal. And I submitted to him every single time.

Capone owned me. Always had. Even from the very beginning when our eyes met across that dimly lit bar. The feeling that swept through me—the lust—was still present years later.

Now, it was no longer just the two of us. We had our other men and April. And walking into Rider's room and seeing her practically folded in half with him buried deep inside of her…

Being forced to wait to get off was definitely fucking worth it.

I watched as Rider gripped April's chin, forcing his tongue into her mouth, choking her for a moment since she could hardly fucking breathe as it was. Then, he roughly shoved her face to the side, forcing her eyes to lock on me. They were dazed and filled with lust, her pupils blown. And fuck, seeing her like this… She was goddamn breathtaking.

To anyone else, she might seem like a slut, but she was perfect for us. We were men with high sex drives, and it was one of the reasons we agreed to be together. But having a woman to share between us as well was fucking amazing. And knowing she belonged to all of us, that all of us would go above and beyond to protect her, settled all of us in a way nothing else really ever could.

And getting to take care of her, having her trust us, was something none of us would ever take for granted after all the shit she went through with her abusive asshole of an ex. Just the mere thought of him and what he did to her was enough to make my molars grind together. I had to force my jaw to relax. Both she and Rider were quick to pick up on my mood changes.

I'd hate myself a little if I killed the mood in the room.

"His turn, my girl," Rider whispered against her cheek. Her skin flushed a shade darker as she trailed her eyes over me, drinking me in. A shiver wracked through her frame. Rider winked at me, leaning up from her the slightest bit to better run his eyes over me. A shiver raced down my spine. I loved the way Rider worshipped me with his eyes. "Who'd you get inside?"

I hummed and reached down, stroking my slick cock. "Capone." Rider groaned. I knew how much he and the other guys loved to watch us together. I moved forward, nodding my head for him to get off of her. "Move. It's my turn." When he slid out of her, her moaning at the loss, I pointed to the bed. "Let her clean you up."

Rider growled in response to being interrupted before he could get off, but he knew I wouldn't let him suffer. I wasn't Capone; I didn't enjoy edging him. I liked to see them all get off so many times, they were crying from the oversensitivity.

Rider chuckled when I gripped April's hips and flipped her onto her stomach before dragging her back toward me so her feet were planted flat on the floor. I kicked her feet apart, baring her swollen, wet pussy to my eyes. Her juices were still dripping from her cunt and running down her thighs.

It was a messy, hot-as-hell sight. It would've looked even better with Rider's cum sliding out of her, but I wanted him to fill her throat.

"You ready for me?" I asked April as Rider shifted so he was in front of her. I gripped her upper arms and leaned her up, allowing Rider to slide beneath her body. As I lowered her back down, she opened her mouth and swallowed Rider to the back of her throat without a second's hesitation. A low growl sounded from my throat at the sight.

The things this woman did were damn near pornographic.

Rider groaned and fell back against the bed, his eyes shutting, but not before I saw them roll back into his head for a moment. April's mouth was fucking sinful, and she could probably suck dick better than any highly-paid porn star.

I gripped my throbbing shaft and slicked the tip up a little more between her folds before easing inside of her. She moaned around Rider's thick cock, and she quickened her pace, bobbing her head up and down, her hand fisted around his base as she jacked him in time with her mouth.

"*God*," Rider groaned, his hands lacing in her hair. I understood the sentiment. Her pussy was choking my dick, strangling it and already trying to pull my orgasm out of me.

I eased out of April before pushing back in, letting her walls adjust to my size. I could be a savage, but I never wanted to hurt her. She wasn't as good at taking pain as the guys. She was the one we were forced to be gentle with, which helped us keep our aggressiveness in check.

"You feel so good, baby," I rumbled, my palms sliding up her back. She whimpered, and Rider cursed, his hands tightening in her hair. She loved it when I praised her, whether it was her body, her pussy, or when she'd done something good. She was such a praise slut, and I couldn't get enough of the way she reacted when she knew we were proud of her.

"Oh, fuck, my girl, I'm so fucking close," Rider rasped, his hips jerking as he drove his cock further down her throat.

I leaned my massive body over April's, placing my lips at her ear. She trembled as my breath fanned her ear. "Swallow everything he gives you, baby. Don't you dare waste a drop."

She worked Rider faster as I eased in and out of her, and when he yelled her name, spurting down her throat, our good girl swallowed all of his cum before popping him out of her mouth. He lay beneath her, panting, trying to catch his breath. April gripped his thighs, her manicured nails digging into his skin as I slowly fucked my cock into her.

"Now it's your turn," I told her. Gripping her hair, I turned her head to the side, licking into her mouth to taste Rider on her tongue. Then, I leaned up and gripped her hips before fucking her harder, driving my cock into her slick, swollen cunt. Her nails broke the skin on Rider's thighs drawing blood as she cried out my name, her pussy already clenching around me.

"Tank, fuck, please," she babbled. Rider sat up, running his fingers through her hair, knowing she was going into sensory overload. She sobbed, tears running down her cheeks. I continued driving forward, chasing my orgasm, and my dick kept brushing against that spot inside of her, my balls slapping her clit, making her come over and over again. Her pussy was strangling my cock, and it felt incredible.

"Fuck, April," I growled. She felt so fucking good. So wet. So warm. Always so fucking needy even when she felt like she'd had too much.

"Tank," she begged, shaking her head. I leaned over her, gripping her shoulders, forcing my weight on hers to keep her grounded as I wrenched yet another orgasm from her tired body.

"So close, darlin'," I soothed, peppering kisses to her shoulder. "You going to let me come inside of you, fill you up?"

On a sob, she nodded, wanting it so badly even while her body was shaking. Rider leaned over her, wrapping his arms around her head as I fucked into her cunt in short, quick thrusts before exploding inside of her. I shouted her name, my eyes rolling back in my head for a moment. Tingles rushed through me, making me lightheaded.

As soon as my balls were empty, I eased out of her, and Rider tugged her up onto the bed. I quickly moved to lay with them, sandwiching her between us.

Capone was standing at the door when I looked over to see if anyone had come to check on her, a frown on his lips. "I heard her crying," he gruffly stated, stepping further into the room, murderous intent in his eyes. My dick threatened to come alive again. Shit, Capone was hot as hell when he went into overprotective mode for our girl.

"She's alright," I assured him as I stroked my hand down her body while she cried into Rider's chest. He gently shushed her. "Sensory overload. She just needs some rest."

Capone kneeled on the bed, and I moved back a little, letting him between me and April. She rolled over, and her eyes slowly opened, glassy with tears. He ran his hand down her naked side as I draped my arm over them both, my hand resting on Rider's hip.

"You okay, baby girl?" Capone asked softly, his hand leaving her side to cradle her tear-stained cheek.

A sleepy smile tilted her lips as her eyes fluttered shut. "So good," she mumbled, sleep dragging her under.

I pressed a kiss to Capone's shoulder blade—right where my name was inked into his skin. "You know we'd never let anything happen to her," I quietly told him.

His throat clicked when he swallowed. "I worry," he said softly. "Worry I'll fail her again." I knew the day he turned her away still haunted him. I had a feeling it always would. My heart clenched in my chest for him.

He thought he was protecting us.

Rider grabbed Capone's hand, linking their fingers together. "No one can fault you for that, Capone," Rider told him quietly, his eyes imploring Capone to believe him. "Even April doesn't. You were trying to protect us from whatever she might have brought our way."

Capone sighed. "Doesn't change the fact that my choices almost got her killed."

Rider squeezed his hand to the point their knuckles turned white against their tattooed flesh. "If she's with one of us but she screams for you, Capone, *then* you should be concerned," Rider told him. I nodded my head in agreement, even though Capone couldn't see me. "Until then, just breathe."

I tangled my legs with Capone's. "Catch a nap with us," I said quietly, shutting my eyes.

"I'm not naked," Capone rumbled, but he settled in, getting comfortable, his hand still joined with Rider's on top of April's ribs.

I chuckled. "We can remedy that," I rumbled, thrusting against his jean-clad ass.

He snorted. "Get some rest, Tank," he said instead.

# CHAPTER 6

*Brewer*

Capone walked his fingers up my bare abs, and a shuddered breath slid from between my parted lips at his sure touch. His other hand slid along my bare thigh, his callouses scraping over my skin. I shifted the slightest bit, and both of us moaned when his dick brushed my prostate.

Christ, he was so deep inside of me. I was so full, and I dreaded the moment I was empty again.

"You're always so fucking tight," Capone hissed as he flexed his abs, forcing himself to remain still. I wanted April with us before we came, and Capone was trying to respect that. I'd spent the night in

Capone's bed, and he'd fucked us both stupid, but this morning, I wanted my connection with my girl before we got off again. I craved her like I was missing a limb.

"If she doesn't hurry up," Capone rumbled, eyeing the door with impatience, "I'm going to take what I want."

My entire body trembled at the sensual promise in his words. A smirk tilted his lips as he locked his eyes back on mine. "You said she had a rough day yesterday," I panted, digging my nails into his abs when he intentionally flexed his cock inside of me.

When I'd heard that, I'd wanted to rush into Rider's room to check on her, where she had still been passed out. But Capone had kissed me to the point I couldn't remember my name and pulled me upstairs to his room. And I'd followed, easily submitting to him, knowing he knew what was best when it came to her.

"She did," he said, shrugging a shoulder, but I could see the storm brewing in his eyes. He hated it when she had rough days. They made him a bit murderous. "Tank and Rider overstimulated her. But I'm not a patient man, Brewer."

I sighed. I knew that. Fuck, none of us were unless it came to April. Most of the time, for her, all seven of us had the patience of a fucking saint. But even I knew when Capone was inside of me like this, his patience with her was thin. The man had an insatiable sex drive, and it was taking every bit of his restraint to not fuck up into me and make me lose my mind.

The door *finally* slowly opened, and April slipped in, shutting the door back behind her with a soft click. When she turned to face us, her breath hitched in her throat, and she licked her lips, her cheeks coloring a beautiful shade of pink.

She had no business being as beautiful as she was. Absolutely none. But at least she was ours, and we could protect that beauty.

"There she is," I rumbled, twisting my upper body with a hiss to hold my hand out to her. She was only wearing one of Tank's shirts, and it swallowed her, the neckline so big that it slipped off one of her shoulders. I bet she would even smell like him, and I licked my lips at the thought.

*Fuck.*

"Strip," Capone ordered as she neared the bed.

Without hesitation, she pulled Tank's shirt over her head, dropping it to Capone's apartment floor before she tugged her black, cheeky panties down her thick thighs. I groaned at the sight of her pale, tattooed, curvy body. Fuck, she was so damn stunning. I had no idea what any of us had done to ever deserve her, but I'd never take having her in our lives for granted.

Sex with her was phenomenal, but her companionship was *everything*. She was so sweet and caring, and she loved all of us in exactly the way we needed to be loved. She picked up on all of our love languages to fucking easily—like it was second nature. I was the kind of man who craved physical closeness, though I didn't like asking for it. And she picked up the signs that I needed to be with someone so damn easily. She knew exactly when I needed her and how.

Even though there were seven of us to take care of her, I still felt like the seven of us together weren't enough for her. She was so fucking selfless, so giving. I knew we owned every single part of her, and I hoped she knew she owned us in turn. The best thing we could give her was ourselves, and fuck if we weren't giving her every piece we had.

"Come here," I rumbled.

She crawled onto the bed, and I lifted her, my ass clenching around Capone's dick. Capone groaned, his eyes shutting, his fingers digging into my thighs so hard, I knew I would have bruises later. I moaned, my hands tightening on April before I forced my grip to loosen so I wouldn't hurt her. "You're going to ride me, but you're going to face Capone," I told her. "He's going to fuck both of us at the same time."

"Oh, fuck," she whispered, her eyes heating, turning to liquid pools of lust. She loved being fucked like this.

I grinned and pressed a hard, bruising kiss to her lips before I spun her around to face the man who owned all of us. Capone smiled at her, his eyes softening for her in a way they didn't soften for us, but none of us took offense to it. We were all hardened men, but she deserved every ounce of tenderness we could give her.

Straddling Capone's abs, she gave me her back. He gripped her hips, and she planted her hands on his chest as I wrapped an arm around her, easing her back on me. She shuddered as I slid into her warm, wet pussy, and Capone trailed his hand up her body before circling her throat. She moaned, and I imagined her eyes were rolling back in her head.

"Come here," he murmured, pulling her lips down to his. He kissed her thoroughly, his tongue probing between her lips. She relaxed for both of us, and gripping her hips, I closed my eyes as Capone began to fuck up into me, which rocked my body forward, making me drive in and out of her.

I hissed a breath through my teeth as I watched through slitted eyes while Capone made out with our woman, lavishing her with attention and love. My chest swelled with emotion as I watched them. I could never get enough of seeing any of my men with April. It filled with me so much fucking contentment, I almost couldn't stand it.

And watching Capone go all soft for her? Fuck, it was nearly orgasm-inducing.

"Fuck," I rasped, my hands sliding over her smooth back. I trailed my fingers down her spine, my eyes rolling back in my head just as Capone hit that perfect spot inside of me. April ripped her lips from Capone's and cried out, her pussy walls clenching around my cock as she came.

"There it is," Capone growled before he gave into his baser instincts and began to really fuck me, driving an orgasm from my body. I spilled inside of April with a shout, and Capone snarled my name, his arms bound tightly around April as he spilled inside of me.

I fell forward, my hand slamming to the mattress to keep from crushing April. Every part of my body trembled from the force of that orgasm. Gritting my teeth, I drew in deep breaths, a low whine spilling from between my lips when Capone eased April off my cock. With a hiss, I moved off of him and fell beside him on the mattress, my chest heaving.

April rolled so she was laying between us. She rested her head on my chest and draped her arm over my waist. One leg tangled with mine, and she sighed when Capone curled around her, his arm wrapping around her waist.

"Did you get enough sleep?" Capone asked her when she yawned. Sex always drained her. It was kind of adorable. But the after-sex cuddles were *amazing*.

She nodded, but her drooping eyes told another story. She honestly probably needed a week of recovery from all the sex, but none of us would last that long without her. Not to mention, she'd go a little crazy without us touching her. She craved us in every way we could be with her.

"Get some rest," I told her softly. Turning my head, I brushed a kiss to her forehead. "I'll stay with you." It was a little selfish of me because I was staying more for me than her, but she didn't care. She flattened her hand along my ribs, letting her eyes stay shut.

"I need to get with Hawke and go over finances," Capone whispered once we were sure she was asleep. "You got her?"

I nodded. He leaned over her and smoothed his lips over mine, dipping his tongue into my mouth for a moment before he slid off the bed. I watched as he yanked his jeans back on and pulled a t-shirt over his head, hiding his body from my hungry gaze. But fuck, the way he looked as he shrugged his cut onto his shoulders… it was porn worthy. The man oozed power, and it called to every submissive part of me.

"Get some sleep, too," Capone told me as he shoved his feet into his boots. "I know you can use the rest, too."

Hell, he wasn't wrong. All of us could use extra sleep, really. But the club called and so did our duties.

I shut my eyes, taking advantage of his order. Rolling onto my side, I circled my arms around April and draped a leg over her thighs, holding her captive. I barely heard the door click shut as Capone left the room.

# CHAPTER 7

*April*

Brewer was curled around me, my head resting on his left arm when I opened my eyes. His right arm was banded around my torso, his face buried in my hair. I yawned, and when I breathed in, the scent of Capone infiltrated my lungs. One glance at the nightstand told me we were still in Capone's bed, though the man himself wasn't in the room with us.

A picture of Capone and I was sitting on the nightstand beside one of his guns, and beside that picture was a pic of him and the rest of the guys. My heart swelled in my chest as I ran my eyes over each face in the photo.

God, I loved all of them so much. They'd given me a home. Safety. Somewhere to finally belong. And while their dynamic had been different to me when I'd come here, I'd quickly fallen in place with them.

Besides, seeing them together... it fucking did something to me. I'd thought something was wrong with me when I was with my ex. My sex drive was basically nonexistent, which led to fights that ended in me sobbing on the floor, blood running down my legs from my ex taking what he wanted because I wouldn't give it to him. But these men had awakened something within me when I'd not only seen them together, but they'd offered their protection to me.

And made my ex disappear.

I would never forget that night.

*My hands flew to my throat, a scream ripping from my lungs. It still felt as if he was ripping inside of me, but the bed was not his. It was my own. Silk sheets covered the comfortable mattress, letting me know I was safe and under protection. Expensive sheets like these would never have been found on my ex's bed. He couldn't afford them.*

*My room door flew open, and all seven men rushed inside the room, weapons drawn. I shrieked and scram-*

bled into a sitting position, scooting against the head-board, my heart thumping wildly in my throat at the sight of those weapons. Vomit threatened to spew from my lips. My heartbeat rattled in my lower front teeth.

Just as quickly as they'd barged in, the weapons disappeared from sight, and Tank and Capone got on the bed. Tank reached for me first, and I fell into his embrace, sobbing out my pain and the horror I'd just relived.

"You're okay," Tank said softly, his fingers running through my long, dark strands. "You're safe now. He can't touch you again."

"It felt so real," I sobbed. "I thought I was right back in that house, on his mattress—" I choked on another sob, my words abruptly cutting off.

"The fuck did you just say?" Capone said softly, but there was danger lining his words. He grasped my chin and turned my head to face him. Murderous intent gleamed in his eyes, but his touch was soft—gentle. "Did he fucking rape you, baby girl?"

My lips trembled, and that combined with the horror no doubt lingering in my eyes was enough of answer for him. He pointed at Smokey and River as he got off the bed. "Both of you stay here with Tank."

"Capone—" I choked out, my hand reaching for him.

*Leaning over the mattress, he grasped my face in his hands and smoothed his lips over mine. "I'm going to make him disappear, baby girl. I promise."*

*With that, he strode from the room. Smokey grasped my hand in his, and River stroked his fingers through my hair. Tank never relinquished his hold on me.*

*"What is he going to do?" I asked, my voice scratchy from screaming.*

*"Exactly what he said he was going to do," Smokey gently told me. Sniffling, I looked at the gentle giant. He brushed his thumb over my knuckles, softly smiling at me. "Get some more sleep. We'll be right here. I promise."*

*I hadn't wanted to fall back asleep, but with the three of them holding me in some form, my eyelids drooped. And I didn't wake back up until Tank gently shook me. When I groaned and burrowed deeper against his chest, he said softly, "Open your eyes, baby. Capone is back."*

*My eyes flew open at that. Sure enough, Capone was standing in front of me. Wordlessly, he set a box on the bed and opened it up for me. Vomit rushed up my throat, but I swallowed it back down.*

*Capone had chopped off my ex's dick. The bloody member was lying in the box, which was lined with plastic on the inside.*

*"Capone," I rasped, raising my eyes to his.*

*He cupped my cheek, dried blood lingering under his fingernails. I covered his hand with mine, a tear running down my cheek. "He's dead, baby girl. He'll never touch you again." Leaning down, he brushed his lips with mine, and another tear ran down my cheek. I circled his wrist with my fingers. "No one will ever get their hands on you again," he swore.*

"You awake?" Brewer rumbled into my hair, his deep, sleepy voice sending shivers down my spine. I blinked, slowly coming out of my head.

I nodded. "Yeah," I mumbled. I rolled over to face him. "How long has Capone been gone?" The last thing I remembered was them sandwiching me between them before I promptly passed out.

Brewer stretched and groaned. "He headed out to do some weapons counts with Smokey and Rider." Brewer pressed a kiss to my shoulder before releasing me and sliding out of bed. I huffed at the loss of his body heat. "Hawke wants to take you on a ride. You up for it?"

I groaned and rolled onto my back, squinting up at Brewer. He was damn good-looking with dark brown curls that flopped over onto his forehead and striking blue eyes. Not to mention all those muscles and those fucking tattoos. All of the men in this club looked damn good. Sometimes, I felt like they were all too good to be true.

A light knock sounded on the door before Hawke slipped through, grinning at me. "You look like you just woke up, doll."

"I did," I mumbled.

He set some of my clothes on the end of the bed before rounding it. Reaching down, he yanked the blankets back, a deep rumble sounding from his chest as he ran his eyes over my naked body. I shivered under his hungry gaze. "You look good enough to fucking eat."

My cheeks flushed. Brewer chuckled. "Not sure she can handle more right now," Brewer warned him.

Hawke rolled his eyes before grabbing me beneath my arms and hauling me out of bed. I whined, not ready to be up yet. Hawke lightly smacked my ass. "Get showered and get dressed. We're going on a ride." Then, he turned to Brewer and gripped the back of his neck, pulling Brewer's lips to his. My sore pussy clenched at the sight of them together. "Hey, babe," Hawke rumbled. Brewer relaxed into Hawke's hold. I loved how Brewer so easily submitted to Hawke, even if Hawke was slimmer and just a tiny bit shorter than him. Hawke just had that way about him—an air of dominance no one could really ignore.

Unless that someone was Capone and Tank, who only submitted to each other.

"Doll, I feel you staring," Hawke rumbled against Brewer's lips. He finally turned his head, looking down at me. "Shower."

I pouted, but he just grinned before backing Brewer up to the bed. I huffed and turned toward the bathroom. I heard Hawke huskily laughing behind me. "And don't you dare touch yourself for that little bit of sass!" he called after me. "I'll take care of you later."

I hated him sometimes.

I was washing my hair when Brewer's moans started. My legs trembled, my body aching for relief, even though Brewer had just fucked me a little stupid earlier in the day when Capone was fucking him. But God, hearing Brewer slowly fall apart was driving me crazy.

"Hawke... *fuck*, baby," Brewer groaned. "God, just like that. Fuck, you suck my dick so good."

I whimpered, sinking my teeth into my lower lip. Wanting to see them together, even if only for a split second, I quickly finished bathing and got out, wrapping a towel around me. I stepped out of the bathroom right as Brewer shoved Hawke's throat all the way down on his thick shaft and came. I couldn't keep back the moan that spilled from my lips even if I tried.

Hawke popped off of him after and licked his lips, grinning wickedly. "Always such a good boy for me, Brewer." Hawke leaned over him and pressed his lips to Brewer's, kissing him softly. "Get some more rest. I've got our girl."

Hawke stood back up to his full height and turned to look at me, arching an eyebrow. "You going to get dressed, April?"

I sighed, rolling my eyes. He *tsk*ed and stepped toward me just close enough that he could reach out and snag the towel from around me. I shivered as he dropped it to the floor, my nipples pebbling. His gaze was intense as he raked his eyes over me.

"Goddamn, you look fucking sinful," he rumbled. Then, he grabbed my black thong from the end of the bed and kneeled at my feet, holding it out. My cheeks colored as I gripped his leather-clad shoulders and stepped into them, allowing him to pull them up my legs. Hawke was a caretaker through and through, and one of the ways he liked taking care of any of us was by picking out our clothes and dressing us. Even Capone and Tank allowed it sometimes. But it was a rare occasion for them.

I'd been tempted to call Hawke Daddy a few times, the word always right there on the tip of my tongue, but I always chickened out. Because if he didn't want to be called Daddy, I would feel like utter shit afterward.

But I wanted that dynamic with him *so* badly.

He rolled my leggings down so I could push my feet through them, and then he pulled them up my legs. A sports bra came over my head next, and then a t-shirt was pulled over that. After, he slid my leather jacket up my arms so it would rest perfectly on my shoulders. The jacket was a gift from him a couple of months ago. He loved having me on the back of his bike, and he apparently loved how I looked in leather.

Some men loved lace. Hawke was all about leather.

He tapped my ass. "Go find Tank and get your boots on." He then pressed a kiss to my lips before gently nudging me toward the door.

I looked around him at Brewer, who was already almost asleep. Hawke chuckled when I pursed my lips in concern. "I'll get him settled into bed, doll. Boots."

I nodded and quickly left the room, but not before I blew Brewer a kiss, which he sleepily pretended to catch and press to his heart. With a smile on my lips, I quickly made my way up the hall to find Tank. He was already waiting on me, my boots resting on the floor at his feet.

"Sit," he gently ordered. I quickly took a seat, and he crouched, sliding my socks on my feet before pushing my boots on, lacing them up so they were snug. "You sleep okay?" he asked me.

I nodded. "Really good." I watched as he stood up and towered over me. "How come you didn't go with Capone, Rider, and Smokey?"

"Needed to be here to keep you safe," he told me with a wink. "You know how things go. If we can avoid both of us going, either Capone or I am always here."

I flushed. "I'm a big girl," I reminded him. "Besides, nothing has happened since I moved in here."

He grabbed my hands in his and pulled me up from the chair. "I know, but we love you and want to protect you anyway." Then, he grasped my chin and pulled my lips to his as Hawke came from down the hall, a smirk curving his lips when he ran his eyes over me, the dark depths of them turning to liquid heat, making me shiver. "Enjoy your ride, darlin'," Tank told me before stepping back and allowing Hawke to take his spot.

Hawke held his hand out to me, and I quickly placed my smaller one in his. "Ready, doll?"

"Yes." I linked my fingers with his, allowing him to lead me out of the clubhouse. "Sorry everyone else has been taking up my time," I apologized, feeling a little guilty now that I thought about it. I'd been denying both him and Smokey of my time, and that wasn't fair.

He chuckled and gently squeezed my hand as we neared his bike. "Doll, you have seven men wanting time with you. Sometimes, that means not all of us get priority, and that's okay. We're fine with that." He gently turned me to face him and reached up to cradle my cheek with his free hand. "And you know why?" he asked, running his thumb over my cheekbone. I shook my head. "Because we also have each other. None of us are left feeling neglected or unloved."

I leaned my face into his hand, closing my eyes. "I love you," I whispered.

He tilted my face up and pressed a tender kiss to my lips. "I love you, too, doll." He then reached over and grabbed my helmet off his seat, settling it on my head. The visor was flipped up, so he could still see me clearly. "We'll ride for a little while, get some food in your system, and then, we'll come back here and put on a show for the guys. How's that sound?"

My cheeks flushed, and my nipples hardened, my core clenching with need. "Sounds great," I whispered, my voice breathless and strangled.

A cocky grin tilted his lips before he flipped my visor down. Then, he straddled his bike, and I quickly slid on behind him, wrapping my arms tight around his torso, my thighs squeezing his hips, just the way he liked me to ride.

# CHAPTER 8

*Hawke*

April's hair was windblown when we got back to the clubhouse, making her look sexy as fuck—like she'd just been thoroughly fucked. It was one of my favorite looks on her.

As soon as I was off the bike and both of our helmets were resting on the seat, I gripped a handful of her tangled, dark tresses and yanked her head back, claiming her lips as my own. I couldn't fucking resist her, even if I'd wanted to. Feeling her behind me the entire ride, the way her thighs squeezed my hips when we took a turn, how her soft breasts felt against my back…

Fuck, she drove me *crazy*. And she wasn't even trying to.

She moaned under the assault, her body easily submitting to mine. Her mouth softened, allowing me to take what I wanted from her. Almost like it was second nature for her to give in to me; she always did it so easily. It was a power she was giving me that I would never take for granted.

I licked into her mouth, tracing my tongue over her teeth before I pulled back to suck her lower lip into my mouth, gently biting down on the kiss-swollen flesh.

She shivered and whimpered, and the sound went straight to my cock.

"Let's get you inside," I rasped. Otherwise, I was going to bend her over my bike, which I couldn't do. Not if I wanted to give our men a show.

She nodded in agreement, her pupils blown wide, her eyes a little hazy with lust. Just how I fucking liked her. April was always beautiful, but when she was in this particular headspace, accepting what we gave her, she was stunning. In this headspace, she didn't have to think. All that was left to do was feel and follow our commands.

I grasped her hand in mine and led her into the clubhouse. The guys were sitting around playing a game of poker, but I didn't give a shit. I swept their cards and chips off the table before laying our woman out on it like a feast. None of them protested. When it came to our woman, nothing else mattered. I knew they'd always choose her over a stupid ass game, no matter who the fuck happened to be winning or how much money had been at stake.

Capone smirked and leaned back in his chair, tracing his thumb over his lower lip. His eyes heated as he watched me get her ready. A shiver raced down my spine. I liked being in charge, but I also loved being beneath Capone or Tank, taking whatever they had to give me. And occasionally, I'd bottom with one of the other guys, letting them fuck into me, but with them, I still gave the orders.

With Capone and Tank, I easily submitted. Letting them take charge was surprisingly as easy as breathing.

And the way Capone was looking at me... No doubt, he had plans for me once I was done with April. That look had me leaking into my briefs.

April's head was right next to Smokey, who leaned in and grinned at her. He traced his fingertips down her neck, and she sighed, her eyes fluttering closed for a moment as she lost herself in the simple sensation of his touch. Smokey wasn't really interested in sex, but that didn't matter. He had a way of bringing us to our knees with a simple touch, like he'd just given April.

"Hey, baby," he murmured.

"Hi," she squeaked. A low groan crawled up her throat when Smokey laid claim to her mouth, tongue-fucking her while I stripped her out of her clothes. Within a couple of minutes, her body was bare, and all of our men were staring at her, unable to rip their eyes away from how fucking beautiful she looked, spread out like this for our eyes to feast on.

"You ready for me, doll?" I rumbled. I shoved her thighs apart before she could answer and swept two fingers through her folds, groaning at how slick she was. "Fuck yes, you are. Because you're such a good girl, aren't you?" I cooed.

She whimpered and nodded. I unbuckled my belt and unzipped my jeans before pulling my cock out, rubbing it between her slick folds. She whined and arched her back, her feet coming to rest on the edge of the table.

God, I loved how much she wanted us.

"So fucking needy," I rasped. Tank rumbled in agreement, his eyes focused on where my cock was pressing against her. "You ready to take me, doll?"

"Please," she begged. "Please, Hawke. Please fuck me. I need you inside of me."

Fuck, I loved it when she begged. Couldn't get enough of it. So needy and lustful. So fucking shameless.

A feral grin curled my lips right before I sank inside of her. Capone gripped her arms and pulled them back. She whined, looking up at him, but he just arched a brow at her. She relaxed under his dominant gaze, trusting him.

I grasped her hips and pounded into her. Her breasts bounced with each stroke, her body trying to move up the table with how hard I was shoving into her, but my grip on her hips kept her in place.

Rider took his cock out and began to stroke it, his eyes locked on where I kept disappearing inside of her body. Who the fuck needed porn when the best thing in the world was right in front of him?

"Oh, please. Yes. Yes. Oh, fuck," she babbled, tears leaking from her eyes. "Hawke," she whined, her breath sawing in and out of her lungs, her chest heaving.

"That's it, doll. Take this dick. You love how much I fill you up," I growled.

She nodded, sobbing, her body writhing on the table as I took what I wanted from her all while giving her everything she needed. She loved how brutal I was, how hard I fucked her, how I used her to get off. But she also knew I would never leave her unsatisfied. I loved the way her pussy fluttered around my cock when she came, like it was trying to milk me dry, sucking me deeper into her body until we could never separate.

"Fuck, woman," I snarled. I dragged her a little closer to the edge of the table, and she gasped when her arms were pulled tight. A little bit of pain mixed in her gaze before it flooded with ecstasy.

God, she was perfect for me.

"You going to come for me, doll? Soak me?" I removed one of my hands from her hip and began to rub her clit. She screamed, her back bowing off the table, sobs wracking her chest right before she exploded all over my fingers and my cock, drenching me and the floor like a perfect little good girl.

"That's it," I praised, chasing my own orgasm now as her walls continued to flutter around me. She was shaking and trembling, her face red and splotchy, yet she'd never looked more fucking beautiful.

"One more time," I growled.

She shook her head, but I was already rubbing her clit again. "Hawke, no, please!" she cried out right before she came again, and this time, I snarled her name, emptying inside of her. Smokey immediately stood as I pulled out of her, and he lifted her from the table, quickly carrying her down the hall to his room to provide aftercare.

Capone chuckled and stood from the table, unfastening his belt. A shiver raced down my spine again when I saw the promise of more in his eyes. I licked my suddenly dry lips.

"Your turn, Hawke." He nodded at the table. "Go on and bend over for me."

I groaned and bent over the wet table, grabbing the other side. Capone slid in behind me, and I gasped when I felt his cool, lubed-up fingers press against my hole. My cheek dropped to the table, my eyes practically rolling back in my head. He wouldn't stretch me much; he never did. He knew I loved the burn. The pain. I fucking *craved* it.

"You ready for me?" he rumbled, one hand coming up to grip the back of my neck, pinning my head to the table. Tank settled his hand over mine, grounding me. Because we both knew Capone was about to make me fucking fly. He always did. With me, Capone was never careful. He tested every limit I had without remorse.

I nodded, and he slid home, both of us moaning at the sensation, even as my ass burned at the same time. My eyes rolled back in my skull, and I lost myself in the way Capone fucked into my body, staking his claim on me. Rider's hand came to rest between my shoulder blades, his cock forgotten.

Capone's strokes were brutal. Hard. He gave no mercy as he chased his orgasm. His hand tangled in my hair, yanking roughly on the strands to pull my head back. His teeth sank into my shoulder, and I shouted in pain. Warm blood trickled over my skin, and he took his teeth out of my skin to lick it up before biting me again.

"Fuck," I gasped, my cock aching. "Fuck. Fuck. *Shit*!" I roared when he dug his nails into my cock. My eyes rolled back in my head as I exploded all over the floor, painting the dark floorboards with my cum. Pain exploded behind my eyeballs, over-sensitivity wringing me out and making me bone-less. My shoulder throbbed. A tear ran down my cheek when Capone raked his nails over my balls. I whimpered. "Hurts," I rasped.

"You know your safe word," Capone reminded me.

I trembled, and he shoved two fingers into my mouth to choke me when he strangled my balls in his tight grip. I screamed around his fingers, chok-ing, saliva dripping down my chin.

"Fuck," I heard Brewer hiss.

"He's okay," Tank murmured. "Capone will never hurt him more than he can handle."

"Come for me one more time," Capone murmured in my ear, his voice husky. "You're such a good boy for me, aren't you, Hawke?"

I nodded, snot running down my face. "The best," I choked.

A knife appeared in my vision before he pressed it to my chin, nicking my skin. I swallowed thickly, making a gargling sound when he pressed the blade in further.

I shattered. My eyes rolled back in my head, and a scream tore from my lungs as I came again. Everything hurt. A man wasn't made to come that many times within the span of *minutes*.

Capone snarled my name, dropping the knife, and came inside of me, pumping his cum into my sore hole. Once he was empty, he wasted no time in pulling out and turning me around, scooping me into his arms.

"You're alright," he soothed, his hand running down my spine.

"Hold on," Tank grunted. He reached between us and fixed Capone's jeans. "Now go."

Capone swept me up the stairs as if I barely weighed a thing. My head was so fucking hazy. I laid it on his shoulder, relaxing into his hold.

I was a dominant man. But Capone had a way of breaking me down so easily to the point I relied on him.

# CHAPTER 9

*Smokey*

**M**ornings were my favorite time of day —right when the sky lightened and chased away the dark. It showed me that no matter how dark life may get, something would come along and brighten it for me.

It'd kept me sane when I'd spent *months* in captivity, being sold for men and women to play with as if I were nothing more than a toy on the shelf at a store. As if I weren't a human being with a beating heart and feelings.

I pulled the blunt back up to my lips, taking a long drag, letting the smoke settle in my lungs. I heard the clubhouse door open, but I didn't turn to see who was coming to sit with me. It was rare I got to be out here by myself, but I never minded the company, especially since I knew it would either be April or one of the men.

All of them were welcome to share in my silence with me.

I smiled at April when she appeared in front of me. Without a word, she straddled my hips and pulled the blunt from between my lips, taking a hit for herself. Humming "Bad Habits" by Nerv softly under my breath, I traced my palms up her bare thighs as I watched the smoke curl from between her parted lips. She was barely wearing anything. Honestly, if we let her, I firmly believed she'd walk around naked.

The April we'd known when she'd first come here would've never. Hell, that April preferred to be as clothed as possible. But she'd blossomed under our love and attention, and she'd grown into herself. Learned to accept herself and the love we showered her with.

"One of these days, someone is going to come onto this lot to speak to Capone or Tank, and you're only going to be sitting here in just one of our t-shirts," I rumbled, pressing a tender kiss beneath her ear.

She shivered, and I could see her nipples pebbling beneath my plain white t-shirt. She *never* slept in her own clothes. It hadn't taken us long to learn the pajamas we'd purchased for her were nothing more than a waste of money.

Besides, seeing her in our clothes... we *definitely* weren't complaining.

She shrugged at me and held the blunt out to me after she took another hit. I watched as she let the smoke settle in her lungs before she slowly blew it out, letting it swirl around us. "I don't care," she told me, her voice a little raspy. "There's seven of you. If someone's stupid enough to do something, I know all seven of you will make them pay."

She sure as fuck wasn't wrong. I might have come from a bad background, but I protected those I loved. And I loved her and the six men that kept me safe. That had given me a home and loved me unconditionally despite all my trauma and me not being able to be with them physically.

I settled the blunt between my lips before tugging April even closer, smiling a little when her wet pussy settled against my abs, but I didn't say anything. I just enjoyed the comfort of having her close to me.

Unlike the other guys here, I didn't have a high sex drive. In fact, I barely even had one. I couldn't remember the last time I'd gotten hard. I craved companionship—just spending my time with someone. The guys had never made me feel like shit for it. I enjoyed watching, kissing, touching. But the actual art of sex? It just…wasn't my thing. Sometimes, I wondered if I was broken, but every time I opened up about that, the guys and April shut it down, promising there was nothing wrong with me.

April trailed her fingers down my chest, sliding her fingers through the hair on my chest. I shivered under her touch. My dick was still soft, but that didn't mean I didn't enjoy having her touch me and caress me. And she knew that. I *loved* just having someone touch me like this. There was nothing expected of me. I could just soak it all in without any of them expecting something in return.

Capone had offered to put me through therapy in case my lack of a sex drive was trauma-related, but I declined the offer. I didn't want to open up about what happened to me again. Not that the guys hadn't been able to figure it out for themselves when they found me, but I'd told the club what happened to me about a year after I'd been rescued.

I didn't want to trauma-dump on a complete stranger, even if that was what they were there for. There was no sense in ripping open those wounds again. April only knew because I'd given Capone and Tank permission to tell her, and the only reason I had given that permission was because I didn't think it was fair that she didn't know why one of her men would probably never have sex with her.

Just as I knew what had happened to her and all the hell she went through, she deserved to know what happened to me, too.

I'd been a sixteen-year-old kid when Capone and Tank had taken down the sex-trafficking ring I'd been thrown into when I was twelve. It was bid night once again, and I was on the stage, my hands bound in front of me. I'd been on my knees, my head bowed in submission. I was completely naked, cum leaking out of my ass. The last man who'd purchased me had given me back just in time for me to be put on the stage again. Bruises were littering my body, and a chain was wrapped around my neck like a collar—just tight enough to hurt when I swallowed—and there was a bar on the front of it that named me five-six-two.

Tank had quickly gotten me off the stage as Capone and the rest of the club took out everyone in that room. I'd been shivering, terrified of the big, muscular, tattooed man that was carrying me out of the room. Tank had cradled me against his chest, but it didn't stop my teeth from chattering. He'd done his best to soothe me, but it hadn't really helped.

He brought me straight to the clubhouse and proceeded to get in the shower with me, bathing me until I managed to tell him I felt clean again. It wasn't until I realized he truly didn't mean me harm that I began to trust him a little bit. Without a single word, he'd tugged one of his shirts over my head after our shower and laid down with me in bed, holding me. I'd fallen in love with him that night.

It'd been the first time in four years that I'd felt safe. The first time in four years that a man touched me and didn't want to hurt me. And when Tank realized weed calmed me, he'd name me Smokey because I refused to tell anyone my real name.

I didn't want to remember it. Tank now knew it was Gage, but he agreed to keep it to himself. *No one* else knew. Not even Capone. It was the only thing Capone didn't push for.

Tank and I had bonded that night, and even now, I was a little closer to him than I was with the other guys and even April. But none of them were upset over it. They understood.

Tank and I had formed a trauma bond. And that was much different than the bond I shared with everyone else.

"I lost you for a minute," April murmured, trailing her lips over my jaw.

I turned my head, capturing her lips with mine. She smiled into the kiss. "Sorry, baby," I whispered. Her tongue tangled with mine for a moment before I pulled back, pecking the tip of her nose. I brushed my hand up her back beneath the oversized shirt she was wearing, and she shivered, arching her back to press her breasts against my bare chest.

"I love it when you touch me like this," she said softly.

I hummed and handed her the blunt, letting her take another hit. When she did, she gripped the back of my neck and pulled my lips to hers, letting the smoke curl into my mouth. I growled and kissed her a little harder, inhaling the smoke into my lungs before I softly blew it back into hers.

"That's hot," Tank rumbled from next to us, making April jump.

I pulled back from April and blew the rest of the smoke out of my mouth as I looked up at him. "Mornin'," I rumbled.

He gripped my chin and pulled my lips up to his, kissing me soft and slow. My chest ached at his gentle touch, and as if April sensed it, she slid her hands over my chest, pressing her palms flat over the rapid beat of my heart.

Without a word, Tank settled himself behind me on the picnic table and wrapped his thick arms around both me and April, holding us. He rested his chin on my shoulder, smiling at our woman. "You look pleasantly high," he teased her.

She giggled and leaned forward to seal her mouth over his. He growled, his fingers bunching in the back of her shirt. I felt his cock press against my back in response to her heated kiss before he gripped her messy, dark hair and forced her head back. She whined, but I knew Tank wasn't looking for sex right now. He just wanted company.

"When's church?" I asked Tank as I went back to running my fingers over April's responsive body.

"Whenever Capone and Hawke get out of bed," Tank told me. He nuzzled my neck, pressing kisses to my skin. "You know how rough he and Hawke get. Going to take Hawke a minute to come back to us."

I understood. It was the submissive headspace. We saw April fall into it all the time. Aftercare was extremely important. Not providing it risked a bad sub drop, and while sometimes sub drop was inevitable, we did our best to make it as comfortable as possible.

Hawke hit bad sub-drops all the time, but Capone always brought him back to us.

April frowned at Tank. "Is he okay?"

I trailed my fingers over her back, answering for Tank. "He'll be okay, baby," I assured her. "You know how it is."

She nodded, looking a little sad on Hawke's behalf. "It can suck."

I pressed a kiss right beneath her chin. "I know," I softly told her. Tank pressed another kiss to my neck, making me shudder. He knew I knew. Sometimes, when I woke up from nightmares, he was already there, somehow sensing I needed him. Ten years later, it still felt like I was sometimes trapped beneath men and women, tied up, and being sold.

"Have either of you eaten yet?" Tank asked out of the blue.

I shook my head. "Got up and came to smoke," I told him. It was my morning routine. I had to have my routine. He knew that.

He hummed. "Come on. I'll go make some breakfast. You both need to eat."

April stood up, and I slid off the picnic table next. Tank grabbed April's hand in his before pressing his hand to my lower back, leading us both inside. I didn't protest. I liked it when Tank took over like this. He could be gruff, and his size was definitely intimidating, but he loved fiercely and took care of all of us.

"Both of you sit," he commanded, pointing to the table Rider and River were sitting at. Rider was running his fingers through River's hair, and the younger guy had his eyes closed, his head resting on Rider's shoulder. "I'll make you some breakfast."

"What about us?" Rider grumbled from the table, taking a sip of his coffee.

Tank rolled his eyes. "Get off your lazy ass and make some, boy."

Rider rolled his eyes too before heaving a sigh and standing, taking the command for what it was: get in there and help him cook. He leaned down and pressed a kiss to River's lips before heading into the kitchen.

I grinned at his grumpy face, settling April on my lap again, craving the comfort I got when I was in her presence. Turning, she straddled my lap and twined her arms around my neck, resting her head on her arm. I brushed a kiss to her forehead before shutting my own eyes, listening as the guys all slowly started to wake up.

Hawke and Capone came down the stairs first. Hawke looked tired, his eyes just a little vacant. Capone had their fingers twined together, and he led Hawke over to our table, forcing him to sit before he crouched in front of him, running his fingers over Hawke's cheek. "Let me get you some coffee," Capone rumbled. "Just sit right here, okay?"

Hawke just nodded before closing his eyes. I nudged him with my foot, and he looked up at me as Capone walked away. "You good?"

He nodded his head, but I could tell it was a lie. He was struggling this morning. "I'm here if you need me," I murmured.

He just nodded again. Capone came back to the table with a steaming mug of coffee. "Come on, boy," Capone rumbled. "On your feet. Back upstairs."

Hawke stood to his feet, and Capone gripped the back of his neck, leading him back to the staircase. April frowned after them. I brushed my fingers over her back. She worried about all of us so much. "Capone is taking care of him, baby. He's never let you down; he won't let Hawke down either," I promised her. I brushed a kiss to her temple. "Relax. He'll be fine."

She sighed and rested her head back on her arm, her face tucked into the side of my neck.

# CHAPTER 10

*Smokey*

I brushed my fingers through April's hair, glancing down at her for a moment before focusing back on the TV across the room. She was sprawled over my chest, her lips softly parted in sleep. We'd only come into my room to watch a movie, but within thirty minutes of the movie being on, she passed out. I knew the other guys had a habit of wearing her out when she was with them, and though I knew she loved being the center of their attention, she also didn't get near enough sleep or rest because she wanted to take care of all of us in turn.

She was such a giver. So much so that she tended to forget to take care of herself, too. But that's why she had seven of us to look after her. We did our best to make sure she didn't overdo herself.

A light knock sounded on my door. I turned my head the slightest bit to look at it before I grunted in acknowledgment. It slowly opened to reveal Tank's massive frame. Capone and Hawke were still holed up in Hawke's room, and I was pretty sure the others were outside doing shit to their bikes. I thought Tank would've been outside, too, but apparently not.

Today was a relatively calm, unproductive day. Which all of us desperately needed. No sales. No runs. Just family time.

"She okay?" Tank quietly asked as he rounded the bed. He toed off his boots and peeled his shirt over his head, revealing all of those thick muscles and his tatted skin. I ran my eyes over him. To anyone else, his size might have been intimidating. It sure as hell was for me at first. But now, his size just made me feel safe. Protected. Like nothing in this fucking world could touch me when he was near.

"She's okay," I rumbled. Brushing my hand down her spine, I pressed a kiss to her forehead. "Just tired, I think." I smirked up at him. "You guys take a lot out of her."

He chuckled as he shucked his jeans and peeled off his socks. "She loves it."

I laughed a little, being careful not to jar her. He wasn't wrong about that. I'd never known a woman who loved sex as much as April did.

Tank peeled off his socks and then slid under the blankets. When he pressed his body to April's back and wrapped his heavy arm around both of us, I shivered, my eyes sliding shut for a moment.

Being in Tank's arms was the safest I'd ever felt. Would ever feel, to be honest. I loved the other guys to fucking bits and pieces, but nothing was equal to Tank holding me like this.

"You been doing okay?" Tank asked me.

I opened my eyes in surprise. His dark ones locked on mine. Warmth spread through my chest and relaxed my limbs. His thumb brushed over my hip. Clearing my throat, I nodded my head. "Yeah," I rasped. "I'm okay. Nightmares are still pretty infrequent."

A small smile tilted Tank's lips. "Good. I worry about you."

I sighed, even while my heart felt like it was going to grow wings and burst straight from my chest. "If

I ever start spiraling, Tank, you will be the first to know. I promise." I let a small smile tilt my lips. "There's no need to worry."

He grunted. "I always worry, baby." My heart skipped a beat in my chest. I wasn't much of one for terms of endearment—had been called various forms of them over the years while I was a sex trafficking victim—but from Tank, they heated my soul. He had a way of making the endearment tenderly slide across my skin before sinking into my bones, warming my chilled soul.

April moaned quietly and shifted a little, her arm coming up to rest on my chest. Her fingers clamped on my chest hair, and I bit back a wince all while I softly smiled down at her. She was so clingy, but I couldn't get enough of it. The other guys would cuddle her in a heartbeat, but most of them sent her in my direction, knowing intimate touch like this without sex was my love language.

And this beautiful woman never took offense to them sending her to me. She understood. Knew all of us so well. Had learned each of our quirks, our love languages, and what shaped us so effortlessly. And she loved us as if it were as easy as breathing.

"So glad I don't have chest hair," Tank chuckled, eyeing my chest. I snorted and rolled my eyes. "Does it hurt?"

I shook my head. "It does when she first grabs on but the pain quickly ebbs," I assured him. "Besides, I like it."

He snorted. "You fucking would."

I just grinned at him. He brushed his lips to the back of April's head, his eyes still steady on mine. "Capone was worried about her earlier because she saw Hawke like that. No matter how many times she sees him go through sub drop with Capone, she worries too much every single time."

"Capone has never and will never leave any of us alone during sub drop or any kind of low," I said quietly. I'd even had Capone cuddle me and take care of me once when Tank was gone on a run. I hadn't been out of my room all day, and he found me shaking on the shower floor, icy cold water beating down on me. He'd stepped into the shower fully clothed, turned the water off, and silently wrapped me in a towel before carrying me to bed.

*"I've got you, Smokey," he rumbled. "I'll never let anything hurt you again, you hear me? I'll slaughter*

*anyone who does. You're safe. I'll protect you with my life."*

*"Can't escape it," I rasped, my icy fingers digging into his shoulders. Capone didn't even flinch. He just clutched me tighter to his wet chest and gently set me on the bed. I reached for him, terrified to be by myself now that he had come for me. My thoughts were too dark, my memories too terrifying to relive on my own. I needed him with me.*

*"Don't—" I choked out.*

*Capone cupped my face in his hands. "Easy," he murmured. "Breathe with me, Smokey. Deep breath in." We both deeply inhaled, and I slowly breathed out when he did. "Again." We repeated it four more times before my heart rate was back under control. He stroked his thumb over my cheek. "I need to get out of these wet clothes, and then we'll lay in bed, okay?"*

*I nodded and slowly released him, my fingers aching for his warmth. A shiver wracked through my body when the air conditioning came on and blew over my cold skin, but I didn't dare move. Felt like any movement without Capone touching me in some way would make all that ugliness in my past come racing back.*

*Capone quickly dropped all his clothes to the floor until he was naked, and then he grabbed my hand. I watched* as he got on the bed, leaning his back against the head-board. When he patted his lap with his free hand, I quickly moved, the towel falling from around my waist. I straddled his lap, my legs on either side of his hips. And then I wrapped myself around him, tucking my face into the curve of his neck.

One would think after two years, I'd be able to handle it, but I couldn't. I still struggled every fucking day. Barely got any sleep at night time. Most nights, I ended up in Tank's bed, seeking the safety I so desperately needed wrapped around me.

"You're safe, Smokey," Capone murmured, his calloused hands running up and down my back. "If anyone dares to come for you, I'll slaughter them. Rip their fucking throats out. I know you and Tank are close, but all of us here will go to fucking war over you."

A tear ran down my cheek. "I love you," I croaked.

Capone shivered. It was the first time I'd voiced those words to him and the first time I'd said those words to anyone but Tank.

Capone gripped a handful of my hair and gently pulled my head up. He ran his eyes over my face. "I love you, too," Capone rasped. "I'll gladly fucking bleed for you, boy."

All day that day, he laid in bed with me, forcing water down my throat and my favorite comfort foods—lemon cake, jalapeno jerky, and applesauce. We watched stupid cartoon movies that were just funny and comforting, and he held me until I came out of my funk, never once leaving me alone.

Capone was a hard ass. He was easily one of the most dangerous men I'd ever met. But he loved each of us deeply. And that day was the first day I'd witnessed how deep his love for me went. He had club business that needed his attention, but he shoved it all to the side to take care of me.

I now had his words tattooed on my back: *I'll gladly fucking bleed for you.*

"Lost you for a minute," Tank murmured. I blinked, not realizing I'd gotten so deep in my head. He chuckled. "Thinking of Capone?"

I nodded, my cheeks warming the tiniest bit. Tank raised his hand and brushed his fingers over my cheekbone before draping his arm back over me and April again.

"He'll probably come snatch April from you when Hawke is doing okay again."

Fuck, if I thought Capone loved me deeply, it was nothing compared to how deeply he loved our woman. And I was perfectly okay with that. She deserved *everything* good in this world. And one of the best things in this universe was Capone's adoration.

I chuckled and looked down at our woman who was still peacefully sleeping. "I don't think she realizes how much we all love her," I said quietly.

Tank hummed. "Some could say the same for you, baby."

Though I could feel his eyes on me, I couldn't bring myself to look at him, his words hitting too close to home. He just slid his hand fully over my hip and clamped down, his touch saying everything he didn't voice out loud.

# CHAPTER 11

*River*

April walked outside in nothing but one of Smokey's t-shirts, rubbing at her eyes. A soft smile tilted my lips as Capone and I looked over at her. She'd been napping most of the day in Smokey's room. Smokey was her safe place to recover. I knew all of us took a lot out of her. So, when she was with Smokey, none of us bothered her except to check in on her.

"Hey, tat," I called, drawing her eyes over to us. She had a rolled blunt in her hand, and I chuckled. It wasn't her normal time of the day to smoke, but I sure as hell wasn't one to judge. I'd just gotten done smoking myself. No doubt, Smokey had rolled it up for her before letting her come outside. He was the best blunt roller out of all of us.

She made her way over to us, and Capone reached out, gripping her hips to lift her onto his lap. She placed the blunt between her lips, and Capone used his lighter to light it up for her. Once her blunt was lit, his hands smoothed over her bare thighs. I watched, mesmerized, as she inhaled, allowing the smoke to settle in her lungs before she slowly blew it out.

Fuck, she was so hot when she did that.

A shiver raced through her body when Capone lowered his head, nuzzling into her neck. She turned her head to look at me, and without needing to be prompted, I leaned forward and opened my mouth over hers so she could blow the smoke she was ready to release between my lips. I let it settle in my lungs before I blew it out, fanning hers and Capone's faces with it.

"No panties?" Capone rumbled, pressing a kiss to her throat. I looked down, and my throat clicked when I swallowed as he bared her to my hungry gaze. Her pussy was pretty and pink, ready to be devoured and used. And my dick was raring to be inside of her. Even now, it jerked in my sweats, precum leaking from the tip.

She shook her head in answer to Capone. I moved off the table top and to the seat between her and Capone's legs. A pleased rumble sounded from Capone's chest as he hooked her thighs on either side of his, spreading her open for me. I flicked a wicked smirk up at her before I burrowed my face between her thighs, licking at her wet core.

She moaned, the fingers of her free hand lacing in my hair. Groaning, I licked into her, loving the sweet taste of her. Capone raised her shirt over her torso before pulling it off completely, baring her beautiful body to our hungry eyes.

My dick hardened even more, achingly so, and with a hiss, I reached down, wrapping a hand around my shaft in my sweats. Capone's eyes fixated on my hand with a hungry gaze. "Stop," he growled.

I immediately stopped everything I was doing, and April whined. I glanced up at her from beneath my lashes, watching as she shook her head. "No. Please," she begged, trying to force my head back to her center. I chuckled. I loved how needy she got for us. And while I'd love to please her, make her shatter and come all over my face, Capone had given an order, and I wouldn't disobey him.

"Stand," Capone ordered her as he moved her legs. I instantly grasped her hips to hold her steady as she stood with a foot on either side of my hips. Her pussy was so close to my face, and it took a hell of a lot of restraint to not tease her clit with the tip of my nose, to inhale her addictive, tantalizing essence.

Capone pulled his thick, throbbing shaft out of his jeans, and I groaned, licking my lips. I didn't know who I wanted to taste more—April or Capone. Both were so damn addicting. Capone ran his hand along the curve of her ass before smacking the flesh, making her squeak. I tightened my hold on her hips when she jumped in surprise. "Sit on this fat cock, baby girl," he rasped.

*Christ*.

She rested her hands on his spread knees, and I watched with hungry eyes as she eased her sopping core over his impressive member. Pain pinched her expression for a moment when he began to stretch her. She drew in a deep breath, and as she slowly released it, she settled herself on him completely.

Damn, she took dick so well.

"Good girl," Capone praised. He grabbed her blunt from where it'd fallen on the picnic table and settled it back between her lips. Then, he looked down at me. "Now continue," he rumbled.

My chest heaved as I leaned forward and flicked my tongue over her clit. She mewled, trying to raise her hips, but Capone spread her open just like before and clamped his hands on her hips, keeping her still for me. She gasped, her back arching. No doubt, the changed angle made him feel like he was so much deeper inside of her.

I licked the little bit of his dick that I could, making Capone shudder, before I began to feast on her clit. My right hand circled my shaft, and I moaned against her core, my other hand coming up to roll Capone's balls. Capone snarled and licked a line along April's neck as he began to fuck his cock up into her eager little hole. She whimpered and moaned, the blunt falling from her hand as she lost herself in what we were doing to her. Her nails dug into my scalp, and I shivered at the pain that rolled down my spine. I loved it when she got a little rough, especially since it wasn't in her nature to do so.

The blunt began to roll off the table, and I quickly caught the blunt before it could hit the ground, ignoring the burn as the cherry hit my palm, and set it back on the tabletop before going back to jacking off. She began to shudder, drawing so close to the edge but unable to tip over quite yet. My balls drew up tight against my body, and I licked at her cunt faster, tugging on Capone's balls in the way I knew he liked, and somehow, we all came at the same time, April's cry shattering the peaceful silence outside.

I rested my forehead on her thigh as I spurted into my palm, my chest heaving. Capone laced his fingers in my hair, scraping his blunt nails against my scalp as he softly kissed April, gently working us both down.

No words were needed. Sometimes, the intimacy of these moments after orgasming was all we needed to communicate. And fuck if Capone wasn't the absolute best at taking control of them.

# CHAPTER 12

*Hawke*

April rested her head on my shoulder as I forked a piece of steak and raised it to her lips. Obediently, she opened and closed her mouth over the fork. I slid the utensil free from her lips, and she chewed happily, her eyes closed. I loved taking care of her like this, and I needed it after the night Capone and I had. It took me a little longer than usual to recover from the intense scene we'd partaken in. The sub-low hit me hard.

While he and Tank could switch, I was the one Capone went to when he needed something darker. Even now, my back twinged with pain from the cuts Capone had sliced into my flesh. But I'd begged for the pain. I'd pleaded with him to make me bleed for him. And Capone had delivered.

Fuck. The sub-low and the pain afterward were absolutely worth being fucked with Capone using my blood as lube. Had anyone walked into my room, they would've thought someone had been murdered. The sheets had to be burned out back, and I was pretty sure my mattress might need to be trashed, too.

Honestly, I'd just been fucked how I really wanted to be. Capone saw the darkest parts of me and never batted an eye. Because he was just as fucked up as I was. And he loved every screwed up piece of me as if I were absolutely perfect.

Coming from an abusive family had lent me its own trauma, and it twisted my needs up into something sinister.

Capone had been the one to find me sitting at a bus station, ready to leave this fucking state on my eighteenth birthday. I was battered, could barely stand due to my broken ribs, and I was malnourished. He'd walked right over to me, ripped the bus ticket up, and offered me his hand.

*"Are you out of your fucking mind?" I growled, glaring up at the beefy, thick man standing in front of me, his*

hand outstretched as if he hadn't just basically ripped up a hundred dollars worth of money I'd busted my ass to save. "You just basically trashed one hundred dollars, asshole."

"I'll give you five if you come with me."

I barked out a cruel laugh. "Right. Because kids like me should just follow random strangers when they offer some creepy shit like that."

He crouched in front of me then and pointed to a man leaning against the wall. The man was thickly muscled —built like a fucking tank. His eyes were dark but kind as he stared at me from across the room. He was also extremely fucking hot. "You see that man over there? He's waiting on us. His name is Tank, and he's my vice president."

"Tank." I snorted. "Fits him." I looked back at the gorgeous, tatted man still crouched in front of me. "Who are you?"

"My name is Capone. I'm the president of a small club called Chaos Keepers MC. I got a call from the lady behind the counter, telling me a kid might need a home. We came directly here. So, what do you say? You want a safe place to live where I won't let a single mother fucker touch you ever again?"

*I swallowed thickly. That sounded amazing, actually. Safety. God, had I ever known what that felt like? Living with abusive parents had traumatized me.*

*"Promise you're not pulling my leg?"*

*Capone pulled a weapon out of his cut and placed it in my hands. My face paled a little. "If I try something shady or Tank does, shoot us."*

*I blinked. I'd never held a gun before. My eyes darted around the room, but no one was paying any attention to us. Blowing out a soft breath, I handed it back to him. "I'm trusting you."*

*Capone smiled then, and fuck, the beauty of it blinded me. "It'll be the best decision you ever make in your life," he promised me.*

"I'm full," April told me, suddenly breaking me out of my thoughts. She'd already eaten her baked potato and half of her steak. It was more than I thought she'd be able to eat considering she rarely ate much at one time. She had mini-meals throughout the day, usually. She turned her head so she could look up at me. "Can we shower yet?"

I chuckled and pressed a kiss to the top of her head before passing her off to Brewer, who'd been waiting to get his hands on her. She settled on his lap, and he wrapped an arm around her, dropping a kiss to the top of her head. "Soon," he answered her for me. "Everyone has to finish eating first."

"Everyone?" she asked in confusion as I passed her remaining steak to Tank, who normally polished off her plates for her. He took it with a nod of thanks. "Why everyone? It's just a shower."

I smirked at her and reclined back in my seat, spreading my legs. She licked her lips before focusing her eyes back on mine. Fuck, she was needy. "Because we're joining you, doll."

Her eyes widened. Excitement lingered in their depths. I flashed her a wicked grin. Brewer kissed her throat and ran his hands under her shirt. She shuddered, her eyes fluttering closed.

"You two," Capone spoke up, pointing his fork at me and Brewer, "get her horny ass in the shower. We'll join once we're done."

We sure as fuck didn't have to be told twice. Brewer stood and swung our woman up into his arms, cradling her to his chest as he carried her down the hall to the last room, which we'd turned into a massive bathroom once all of us started fucking around with each other. We enjoyed taking showers together, but it was hard to fit all of us into a small tub or shower cubicle.

So, this entire room had been tiled from floor to ceiling with multiple drains and shower heads. There was also a sink and a toilet, but I didn't think they'd ever been used. They were there just in case anyone happened to need it for whatever reason. But every room had its own bathroom attached.

I stripped out of my clothes in the hallway, while Brewer worked on stripping April until she was as naked as I was, her breasts hanging heavy, her nipples hardened into sweet, little points. Groaning, I stepped forward and took her from him so he could get undressed, too. Bending my head, I sucked one of those dusky nipples into my mouth and suckled. A low, keening sound ripped from her throat.

Water suddenly burst from all the shower heads, and then Brewer was behind her, his hands running over her body. She moaned when he dipped his fingers between her thick thighs, rubbing her clit. Her head tipped back against Brewer's shoulders, revealing that long, slender throat I liked to cover in my marks.

Switching to her other nipple, I tweaked the one I just abandoned, and she twitched, her back arching. Panting gasps ripped from her lungs, and she rode Brewer's fingers like a little whore.

Such a pretty one though. *Our* pretty whore.

"Fuck, you three make a stunning picture," Rider rumbled as he came up beside me, sliding his hand along my back, tracing one of the cuts. I groaned, pain and tingles rushing up my back. I moved out of his way so he could take over and reached down to stroke my shaft, the shower head behind me beating down on my back, stinging the cuts, giving me the pain I craved. "That's it, my girl," Rider murmured in her ear. "Let Brewer feel you fall apart so I can get in," Rider coaxed.

She shuddered, and with one more stroke, she came undone, crying out Brewer's name. He leaned down and kissed her, and before she could even finish coming, Rider was on his knees, her thighs draped over his shoulders. Capone took over from Brewer and held her up while Rider feasted on her like she was his last meal.

There was something about these men worshipping her that got me all hot and bothered. It was almost as good as being inside of one of them.

"Fuck, fuck, fuck!" she chanted over and over, her chest heaving. Her eyes rolled back in her head for a moment as Rider lapped at her clit before spearing his tongue inside her slit.

River came to stand beside me, and I pulled him in front of me. Gripping his cock in my hand, I began to stroke him, sliding my dick between his ass cheeks in tempo with my hand. His breath shuddered out of his lungs, his eyes fixated on our woman as she shattered under Rider's tongue.

Capone spun her around to face the wall and spread her cheeks apart before spearing his tongue inside her ass. Her head fell forward, her hair blocking the view of her face, but from the erotic sounds she was making, I knew she loved it. Capone could eat ass like a fucking champion. He never failed to make me come untouched every time he ate me out.

Smokey pushed her hair out of the way before kissing across her shoulder. She whined, turning her head to look at him. He just smiled at her. It was *very* rare Smokey joined in on group playtime in any sexual way. He liked seeing her fall apart, and he liked to see us enjoy her. But that was the extent of playtime for him.

"Smokey," she whimpered.

"You're doing so well, baby," he promised, his hand caressing her hair. "So good."

A sob ripped from her throat when Tank suddenly settled beneath her and began to lick at her cunt. Capone groaned when Tank began to stroke him, and both of them went to town on her, eating her out from front to back, working seamlessly together like they did on so much else.

She was full-on crying now, and it was beautiful. Smokey kept petting her and crooning to her, holding her steady when her legs threatened to give out. I worked River faster, and he groaned, his head falling back against my shoulder, his eyes sliding closed. With my other hand, I fondled his balls, and he whimpered, his hips moving in time with my hand.

"Fuck, boy," I rasped, nipping at his shoulder.

Tank growled his pleasure, and I looked up in time to see April squirt all over Tank's face and chest. Capone backed off, his chest heaving, and Tank stood from the floor. Smokey, always knowing what April needed, settled on the floor, his back leaning against the wall, before he drew her onto his lap and spread her thighs with his, nodding once at me and River, who was shaking in my hold, his release close.

"Go on," I rumbled in his ear. "Eat her out, and if you're a good boy and make her come, I'll let you come, too."

He quickly nodded and walked over to her on unsteady legs. Capone grinned at him—a grin that promised painful pleasure later—and River shuddered before he kneeled between her spread thighs.

"No—oh, fuck, yes," April whined, her head slamming back against Smokey's chest. "Yes, yes, yes," she chanted.

She wouldn't last long. She was already so sensitive, so it wouldn't take much to make detonate. But River worked her up like he had to really try. April shattered not even two minutes after he started, and I pointed to the spot beside her when he got up. River obediently moved, kneeling where I told him to, and I took his place between April's spread legs.

"Ready, doll?" I rumbled.

Her chest was heaving, her skin drenched from the water and flushed a pretty red from coming so many times. She was beautiful, her eyes clouded with lust and satisfaction.

"Yes," she whispered, "Daddy."

*Oh, fuck. Fuck. Fuck. Fuck.*

My cock jerked, precum leaking from the tip and dripping to the shower floor.

*Daddy.* Goddamn, I'd cherish that title for the rest of my life.

Growling, I dove between her thighs, intending to reward her for giving me something so beautiful. I didn't take it lightly. I knew her calling me Daddy meant something precious to her. She trusted me to always take care of her, and something in my chest loosened at that.

As I went down on her, I fisted River's cock in my hand, giving it rough, firm strokes. River moaned, his hand covering mine, his hot breath fanning over my arm. Out of the corner of my eye, I could see Tank petting his head.

"Hawke, please. Fuck." April's body began to shake, her muscles tightening around my tongue as she tried to close her legs. Smokey wasn't having it though. She sobbed. "Daddy, please!" she cried.

She squirted again, all over my face and hair, and I licked it all up, not even caring how gross it might seem. I wanted everything she could fucking give me.

River came a moment later all over my fingers, and I leaned back on my knees, licking them clean. April sagged back against Smokey, her eyes closing. I grinned and crouched, gripping her chin in my hand. Her eyes opened to mere slits.

"How was that?" I rumbled.

"Sleepy, Daddy," she whispered, her eyes shutting again. My chest squeezed at that title.

"Let's get her bathed and in bed," Capone quietly said. "Our girl needs some rest. Smokey, you good with taking her for the night?"

"Always," he said immediately, his hands smoothing over her bare, damp body.

Capone and I worked on bathing her with little cooperation on her part, while Smokey hurriedly bathed and washed himself. As soon as she was rinsed, we handed her over for him to dry. When they walked out of the bathroom to go to bed, Capone drew me into his arms and ran his fingers through my hair.

I shuddered, my eyes closing as I sank into his embrace.

"Do *not* take what she just gave you lightly," he rumbled in my ear, his hold on me tightening.

I shook my head. "Never," I rasped.

He pressed a hard kiss to the top of my head before releasing me.

# CHAPTER 13

*April*

I jerked awake, my heart in my throat but beating so fast, I could hardly breathe. Smokey sat up with me and tightly wrapped his arms around me, pressing his hand over my mouth when I got ready to ask what the noise was that woke me up. "*Shh*," he whispered in my ear. I nodded, my skin growing clammy as my anxiety spiked.

Smokey had already heard it—whatever it was. That much was clear.

The banging on the clubhouse doors, which apparently what woke me up, started up again, and I jumped in Smokey's arms. He squeezed me to him with one arm, his other arm resting on my thigh. Something cool pressed to my skin, and when I glanced down, I saw the gun in his hand. My muscles relaxed.

I was safe. None of these men would let anything happen to me.

The banging stopped, and I heard one of the doors swing open. "Who the fuck are you?" Capone snarled at whoever was making all the racket.

"P-please," a woman stuttered. She sounded like she was crying, and my suspicions were confirmed when she sobbed and hiccupped. "I need help," she pleaded.

"Jesus fucking Christ," I heard Tank snarl from right outside of our bedroom door. I snapped my eyes to him. I hadn't even seen him move to stand there, but there he was, all huge muscles blocking the doorway. I could see part of an assault rifle held in his hands as he looked down the hall toward the clubhouse entrance.

These men did not take my safety lightly nor the safety of each other. I could probably place money on Tank not being the only man guarding this room.

"Easy," Smokey rumbled, drawing my attention back to him. "He's protecting us. We're safe."

"Tank?" Capone barked. "Your call, babe."

Tank glanced at us. I knew he was wanting my opinion, but I didn't know what the right decision was to make in this situation. It was the middle of the night, and we knew nothing about her. And while I knew I'd shown up just as this woman had, I was nervous about letting in an outsider.

I understood how my men felt back then. They were trying to protect each other. And now, I wanted to protect them.

Besides, my gut was telling me something was wrong, and it rarely ever let me down. I didn't know if this woman was the problem or if whatever was chasing her was the issue, but *something* was off.

I swallowed thickly, refusing to give a yes or a no. I wouldn't be the reason a woman might get sent away, but something about this didn't feel right to me. It felt like there was danger lurking just around the corner. It made me feel cold, and goosebumps crawled over my flesh.

"She may need real help," Smokey told him quietly, speaking up when I wouldn't. "I'll stick by April. She'll be safe."

Tank nodded once before looking back toward the clubhouse doors. "Let her in!" he called to Capone.

Tank stayed standing in our doorway, refusing to move. "Come on," I heard Capone tell her. "Hawke, get her at that table." I relaxed, knowing he had Hawke with him. Hawke was a force to be reckoned with when it came to any of us, even someone as big and invincible-looking as Tank. He would make sure Capone was safe. "What injuries do you have?"

"Just this cut on my arm, some bruising, and I think my nose is broken." She hiccupped again. I squeezed my eyes shut, pushing those horrible memories away. Memories of when my own ex had beaten the shit out of me—almost killing me. I'd barely made it back to this clubhouse. I'd felt like I was dying, and I didn't want my last breaths to be in a hospital. I wanted to be somewhere I knew I'd be safe.

Smokey nuzzled into my neck, sensing my distress. "Stay with me," he whispered, pressing a kiss to the shell of my ear.

I drew in a deep breath, nodding at him. "I'm still here," I promised.

Tank glanced at us before looking back toward the main room of the clubhouse where we sat around, chilled out, and ate our meals. "Why did you come here instead of the hospital?" Capone demanded to know. I heard Hawke popping open a first-aid kit. Capone had asked me something similar the first time I'd shown up needing help. I'd told him hospitals asked too many questions.

Capone had sent me away, only for me to return on the verge of death. I knew that guilt still resided within him. It was probably the only reason he'd allowed Tank to make the call instead of sending this woman on her way much as he'd done me.

"He'll find me," the woman cried in answer. "Please don't send me back out there."

I swallowed vomit. Tank glanced at us over his shoulder again before coming into the room, his eyes steady on mine. "Who?" Capone demanded to know as Tank set the rifle by the bed and slid onto the mattress beside us. Brewer silently took his spot in the doorway. Tank drew both me and Smokey into his arms. I shuddered.

The woman remained silent. My gut cramped. "Who the fuck are you running from?" Capone snapped, getting irritated that he was having to repeat himself.

"My boyfriend," she blubbered. "He—He—" She sobbed. Chills raced down my spine, but I didn't know if it was because of the painful memories I was struggling to keep at bay or because I could somehow tell there was something amiss. "He thought I cheated on him, and he beat the hell out of me," she cried.

"Something isn't right," I whispered, looking up at Tank.

He frowned at me and brushed my hair back from my face with his thick fingers. "Talk to me," he murmured, making sure his voice didn't carry outside of the room. Brewer glanced over his shoulder at us, obviously hearing us, but he turned back to face what was going on quickly, his rifle held low but ready to be used at a moment's notice.

"I don't know how, but I know something isn't right. I've got this bad feeling that something is wrong," I told him quietly. "Like something is going to happen."

Smokey cupped my cheek, turning my head to face him. "Do you want us to send her away? Because we will, April. In a fucking heartbeat. *You* are what matters. Always. And if you don't feel safe, we'll make her disappear," he promised.

I didn't want to know which definition of disappear he meant: just sending her away or making her heart stop beating.

I shook my head. "If he really did do that to her, then I don't want to be the reason she winds up dead somewhere." Tank and Smokey both flinched, easily remembering Capone sending me away the first time and how I almost hadn't survived. I cupped Smokey's cheek, trying to soothe him. He felt everything so much deeper than the others. Tank ran his hands down my arms, bringing some warmth back into my chilled body.

"Then we'll keep a close eye on her," Tank promised me. He pressed a kiss to my shoulder, and warmth blossomed where his lips touched me. "Both of you get dressed. Let me go talk to Capone."

He slipped out of bed, and Smokey got off the mattress before grabbing my hand in his. Once I was on my feet, he silently led me to his closet, where he dressed me in a pair of his briefs and one of his t-shirts that dropped to my mid-thigh. He pressed a kiss to my forehead before getting dressed in a pair of jeans, a t-shirt, and his cut. Once his boots were on his feet and his weapons were tucked into his cut, he grabbed my hand in his and quietly led me out of the room, our fingers linked together.

The girl looked up at me in surprise when we emerged into the main area, like she hadn't expected me to be there. Tank seemed to catch on, as did Smokey and Capone. Smokey tightened his hand around mine.

Everyone in this town knew I lived with these men, and everyone also knew I was theirs—that they shared me.

Her not knowing meant she wasn't from here. It was a major red flag. Because if she wasn't from around here, she'd traveled far. She had an agenda.

Something was definitely up, and if my men had any chance of finding out what that was, it was clear we would have to play a dangerous game.

I fucking *hated* playing these games.

# CHAPTER 14

*Rider*

When we all saw how Malorie ended up looking at April, I herded our woman upstairs to my room, gun at the ready, while Capone worked on getting her name—which I'd caught on my way up the stairs—and where she was from. Smokey camped out in front of my door, and I knew at least two of the guys were outside keeping watch on the property.

Something wasn't right. Had Malorie been from around here, she would've known of April and our relationship with her. Which meant she wasn't. She'd traveled to come here, and that was suspicious as fuck, especially since there wasn't much on the way here. We were in a small town in the middle of fucking nowhere.

When it came to April, we didn't play fucking games. Her safety was our number one priority. And to get to the bottom of this, we had to play along. Just for a little while, even if we didn't like it.

Secretly, I was hoping one of April's weird dreams would come through so we could nip this shit in the bud quickly. Her bad dreams tended to come true or already be true. None of us had believed her at first until it happened three fucking times. Third time was the charm for us.

The first time, she dreamed Capone would end up in an accident on his bike—that something would run him off the road. We'd soothed her, told her he was the safest driver out of all of us, and he would be okay. But sure enough, two weeks later, a drunk driver careened into his lane, and in order to save himself, Capone flew off the side of the road and into a fucking stream.

The second time, she dreamed River went through some fucked up shit as a kid and woke up crying, wanting to see him and make sure he was okay. When Capone brought him into her room, he confirmed what she feared—that he'd been abused for liking boys, too.

The third time, the one that finally cemented our belief in her gift—or curse, depending on the day someone asked her about it—she dreamed that the clubhouse was going to be raided. And sure enough, two days later, ATF agents came out to the fucking clubhouse and raided our shit, dumping everything all over the floor and destroying the place, only to come up with nothing.

We hadn't been worried about being raided, but the warning had been nice, nonetheless. There was nothing here for them to find. We weren't stupid enough to keep anything near our woman that could incriminate her. She was too damn gorgeous and sweet for prison. Protecting her also meant protecting her from us and the illegal shit we surrounded ourselves with.

The door eased open, and I looked up to see Hawke and Capone slip into the room. Smokey was still sitting in the hall against the wall across from my room. Smokey met my eyes for a moment before Hawke shut the door behind him, blocking Smokey from my view.

"She still asleep?" Hawke whispered.

I nodded as he came around to the side of the bed she was laying on. April had fallen back asleep not long after I got up her up here, thankfully. She didn't need the stress of what we were about to be dealing with.

Hawke ran his hand over her hair before leaning down and pressing a soft kiss to her hairline.

"Malorie was trying to discreetly ask questions about her," Capone whispered, making sure his deep voice didn't carry beyond these walls.

I gritted my teeth, swallowing back the blood-boiling protectiveness that surged inside of me. "You think someone is after April?"

Standing at the foot of the bed, Capone shrugged. "I don't know anything right now, but whatever this woman is up to, she's hiding it well."

Hawke carded his fingers through my purple hair, and a shiver rolled down my spine when he gripped the strands and tugged my head back. "Nothing is going to happen to her," he quietly assured me. "She has seven men protecting her. Seven men ready to die for her. She's safe."

I blew out a harsh breath and looked back at my president—my man who bent over backward to keep all of us safe. "I don't like this, Capone. Should we take her to a safe house, at least?"

Capone shook his head. "If she *is* here for April, we risk bringing more heat by doing that. For now, we try to let April go about her day-to-day activities as normally as possible. But she's never alone. I don't care if she's pissing or taking a shit. Am I clear? I never want her vulnerable."

I nodded once. "Understood," I told him. "I'll stay with her until she wakes up. Just have someone bring some clothes for her to get dressed in, yeah?"

Capone nodded. "I'll bring them myself, along with one of Tank's hoodies. It'll swallow her—"

"But it'll make her feel safe," I filled in. And even though we were going to try to make sure April lived normally while Malorie was here, we knew she was going to catch on quickly. She always did, and when she did, it was going to flip her world upside down. Even if we were doing everything we could to protect her, some of her security was going to be ripped away.

Because the real world we lived in had come banging on our goddamn door.

Capone nodded in agreement before walking around and leaning over the bed. I swallowed thickly when he gripped my chin in his hand. "You be careful, too, Rider. Don't go off half-cocked because she's possibly in danger, understand me?"

I blew out a soft breath, his touch relaxing me. "I won't. I promise."

"Good boy," Capone rumbled against my lips. I trembled as he softly kissed me. "Take care of our woman."

I roughly cleared my throat, my dick half-hard. "Always," I promised, my voice sounding like I'd just swallowed gravel.

He pecked my lips one more time, and then he and Hawke left the room.

# CHAPTER 15

*Capone*

I eyed April as I half-assed listened to Malorie drone on and on about something I didn't give two fucks about. For someone who was *supposedly* shaken from what she'd gone through, she sure as fuck talked *a lot*. The only reason I or one of the guys hadn't told her to shut the fuck up was because we were hoping her rambling would get the best of her and she would let something slip.

Like how she really found us. Because I knew she wasn't from around here, despite what she said. And we weren't known for allowing outsiders in. The only reason she was still here was because of April's conscience. But Tank had let me know she thought something was off, which only put me on guard more.

April was too damn sweet for her own good, and I wished she trusted her gut more. But since we now knew we had a problem, I wasn't letting Malorie out of here until we got to the bottom of this shit and the threat was eliminated.

And the only way Malorie was getting out of here was in a fucking body bag.

Malorie placed her hand on my arm and leaned into me so her breasts pressed against my side. I grimaced and looked down at her, nothing but disgust showing on my features. Something clanged over in the kitchen area, and Hawke snickered. "Oh, boy," he whispered.

I barely had time to look up before April's manicured fingers were wrapping around Malorie's wrist and flinging her hand off of me. Malorie reared back in surprise, and I quickly gripped April's hips, settling her on my lap before she could do something I knew her sweet soul would later regret.

She was too good for violence.

"Sheathe the claws, baby girl," I rumbled in her ear before nipping at the skin of her neck.

"I didn't mean—didn't know—" Malorie stammered.

"We are *all* with April," Tank calmly informed Malorie as he came to my side and reached up to run his fingers through April's hair. He tugged her head back by a fistful of her dark strands and pressed a quick, hard kiss to her lips before looking back at Malorie. "If she feels threatened, she *will* lash out."

It went without saying that all seven of us would back her up one hundred percent, too.

Malorie's eyes were wide with a mixture of shock and wonder. I slid my hand under April's shirt, splaying my palm over her belly. Tank released her hair, and I spun April around, making her squeak in surprise, her hands coming up to clutch my shoulders, her thighs squeezing my hips.

"Hawke, you're with me," I ordered, not looking away from the jealous little vixen straddling my lap. Hawke grunted in answer as our woman's eyes went all hazy. "Someone finish breakfast and bring us up three plates when it's done."

I stood from the chair I'd been sitting in with April wrapped around me, her face buried in the crook of my neck. Her nails dug into the back of my neck, but I welcomed the pain.

Someone had encroached upon her territory, and she needed reassurance. I understood it. If someone had touched her like that, I'd probably have fucked her right in front of them.

I could feel Hawke's presence at my back, and I shivered when he trailed his fingers down my spine as I made my way up the stairs.

"Playing a dangerous game, boy," I warned him, but I had a feeling he was trying to get a rise out of me. It was what he did because he knew I wouldn't hold back on him. If I wanted him to hurt, I'd make him hurt. And the way he craved pain...

My cock throbbed, aching to bury itself inside of him.

Hawke hummed. "I've got a thing for danger, Capone." *Fuck, did he ever*. And I loved indulging him—safely. Always safely. Because I never wanted to *truly* hurt him.

"Don't tease him, Daddy," April said, turning her head so she could look at Hawke with her chin resting on my shoulder. I tightened my grip on her in response, a shiver rolling down my spine.

Fuck, I loved hearing her call him Daddy. It fucking did something to me. Hawke earning the title of Daddy was something...special. Something worth cherishing. Hawke said he understood the depth of the gift she'd given him; I truly hoped he did. It was the best fucking title he could have, honestly.

I wasn't a Daddy by any means, but even I envied him just the tiniest bit for earning something so beautiful and precious.

Hawke chuckled. "Teasing him is half the fun, doll."

"Teasing me will also earn you a spanking with the paddle and lots of fucking edging," I calmly reminded him as I pushed open the door to my room. Hawke groaned. "Now, do you want to continue teasing me, or would you like to be able to come in our woman's tight little pussy while I fuck her ass?" I asked him.

April tightened her thighs around me with a desperate little moan, her hips rolling against my hard cock. Groaning, I eased her down onto the bed and glanced over at Hawke, who had just shut the door and was now waiting on my command. Always such a good boy for me. "Strip, boy."

He quickly began to pull his clothes off. I looked down at April and cupped her cheek, brushing my thumb over the corner of her sweet lips. "You know I don't see any other woman, right?" I calmly asked her. She sighed and nodded, her eyes focused on mine, just how I wanted them. "Despite that, baby girl, I'm so fucking proud of you for standing your ground against her. She intruded on the safe space we made for you, and you had every right to defend that." Leaning down, I brushed my lips to hers. "Such a good girl."

She made a small sound in the back of her throat as she tried to follow my lips when I pulled away. I clasped her hand and placed it over my stiff cock, still confined in my jeans. She whimpered and moaned, her fingers gripping me through the fabric. It took every ounce of my restraint not to fuck into her hand. "For you being so fucking good for me, baby, I won't make you wait. And I'll let you cum as many times as you want. How does that sound?"

"Perfect," she breathed. She let her eyes meet mine again. "Thank you."

*Fuck, she was so sweet. So good.*

I eased her out of her clothes and tossed them to the floor. Once she was naked, I ran my eyes over her smooth, tattoo-covered skin. She was so fucking beautiful. I could stare at her all day and never grow bored. Every bit of her was a master-piece. Something to be worshipped. To be loved and doted on.

People in ancient Greece would have carved sculptures of her.

"Hawke," I rumbled, not removing my eyes from our woman, "undress me."

"Fuck yes," Hawke groaned. He slid behind me and reached around, unsnapping my jeans. I toed out of my boots for him to make it a bit easier when he tugged my jeans down my legs. April's breathing quickened when my cock finally sprang free, and she licked her lips, eyeing me hungrily.

"Just a minute, baby girl," I soothed, palming her thick, luscious thighs. She parted them for me readily, her pretty pink center glistening, more than ready for Hawke's thick cock.

Once I was naked, I grabbed Hawke, tugging him in front of me. He raised his chin expectantly, and I smoothed my lips over his, running my hands over his tatted skin. He was all hard muscle and so beautifully submissive for me. Almost as much as April, but not quite. I wouldn't change him for the world. He gave me that fight I needed out of my boys.

I loved each of my boys in different ways but the amount I loved them was equal. And Hawke enjoyed the rougher side of me, allowing me to love him in a darker way that I couldn't with the others. I could with Tank, but he wasn't submissive for me—wasn't a switch. Not like Hawke.

"Lay on your back so April can be on top," I commanded.

He nodded and laid back on the bed before grabbing April and slinging her on top of him. She giggled before leaning down to kiss him, all while she reached back and wrapped her slender fingers around his thick girth. I watched, hypnotized, as her pussy lips spread, and she slowly impaled herself on him.

I grabbed the lube from off my nightstand and squeezed some onto my fingers before probing at her puckered hole. She tensed before slowly releasing a breath, forcing her body to relax for me.

Hawke rubbed his hands down her back. "You're doing so good, doll," he rumbled in her ear. "Ride his fingers and fuck my cock like a good girl."

With a needy whimper, she slowly began to move, fucking herself on his cock and my fingers at the same time. Gasping moans ripped from her lungs. Hawke clenched her hair in his fists, forcing himself to stay still so she could adjust as I spread her open, preparing her for my girth.

Once I deemed her stretched enough, I slid in behind her and dribbled excess lube on my cock before gripping her hips and easing inside of her. She cried out and then sank her teeth into Hawke's collarbone, making him shout in surprise, his cock instinctively driving up inside of her.

"Oh, God, fuck," she panted, sweat glistening on her skin, a little of Hawke's blood painting her lips. I snarled. It was the most erotic image I'd ever fucking seen. Trembles wracked her curvy body. "So full. Too full," she whimpered.

"You take us so fucking well, baby," I rasped, my hands running over her skin, hoping to soothe her while she adjusted. "Your body was made for this, April. Made to be our pretty little whore."

"Yes," she mewled, her body still shaking between us as I seated myself all the way inside of her. Her nails were clawing at my sheets, and a bead of sweat rolled down her temple. I leaned down and licked it up before moving my lips, capturing Hawke's again. We began to move together, fucking her perfectly and in rhythm like it was second nature.

Her voice eventually faded off. She was too lost in coming over and over again that she lost her ability to form any kind of coherent words or thoughts. She was babbling, tears streaking down her beautiful face as we used her but took care of her all at the same time.

"I'm coming," Hawke gritted. "Capone, babe, please—"

"Fill her up," I snarled. I reached between them and formed a scissor around his cock, my palm rubbing her clit. That did the trick for him, and April screamed as Hawke shouted her name, his cock pulsing inside of her, filling her greedy pussy up with his seed.

I sank my teeth into the back of April's neck and spilled inside of her ass, moaning when she tightened around me. She sobbed, her fingers sinking into Hawke's hair while she buried her face in the curve of his neck. I released her skin from between my teeth and rolled to the side, bringing her and Hawke with me. I wrapped my arms around them both, squeezing April between me and Hawke.

"Please don't slip out yet," she managed to utter just when I was about to. I instantly halted, running my eyes over the side of her pretty face. Her eyelids fluttered, but she lost the fight to keep them open. "Just want to feel you two for a little while," she slurred.

Hawke brushed her hair back from her face and pressed a kiss across her swollen lips—no doubt from her biting them and sinking her teeth into the soft flesh of her mouth. "I'll stay in you forever if I can, doll."

She laid her palm over his heart. "Such a good Daddy," she mumbled before she began to lightly snore.

Hawke swallowed thickly, his eyes running over her face in wonder. No doubt, he was trying to figure out what he'd done to deserve her. We all wondered about it on a daily basis. Men like us weren't meant to be loved the way she loved us.

"She's not wrong," I told Hawke quietly after a couple of quiet moments, nothing but the sound of her soft snores and deep breaths filling the air.

He sighed and shrugged at me, but he didn't move his eyes from her beautiful face. "I'm not perfect, but I'm doing my best."

"That's all she wants," I promised him. I brushed my thumb over the tiny bit of skin on his back I could reach. "I'll be rewarding you for being such a good Daddy to her later."

He sleepily grinned at me before shutting his eyes. They would both take a nap, and that was fine with me. He may be April's Daddy, but I owned them all. And I took damn good care of my possessions.

They knew they were safe here with me. I'd never let a fucking thing in this world touch them.

# CHAPTER 16

*Tank*

"What's our plan here?" I asked, glancing at Capone. We were all sitting around the table in the chapel since Capone had called church early as hell this morning. Shit, it was still dark outside, but I knew why he did—less worry for April. "Something's clearly amiss, and we need to deal with it." I was tired of sitting around on my ass and basically twiddling my fucking thumbs while we waited for something to happen.

Capone grunted in agreement. "Smokey has been doing some digging," Capone told us. I glanced at Smokey. He'd been quiet about that—both of them had. "We have a possible location for Malorie's boyfriend, but we have no idea if he might be alone. Fucker was hard to find, which is even more suspicious." I didn't fucking like this one bit. Someone that good at hiding? They weren't new to this, which made shit even more dangerous. "We'll ride out in a bit before April gets up for the day, so she's not freaking out more than she has to."

And oh, she would. She always did. She *hated* it when we went on runs of any kind—even just a charity run. If we weren't home, she drove herself sick with worry. In her mind, if she wasn't there to take care of us, she could lose us.

It was a trauma response; we understood that, and we did our best to make things easier for her. But runs were inevitable and had to happen.

Capone glanced at me. "Tank, I'm leaving you here with Rider, Smokey, and River. Keep our woman distracted until we get back, and keep Malorie the fuck away from her."

"Understood," I grunted. He didn't even have to add that last tidbit. Malorie wouldn't get within ten feet of her. "And you better be fucking careful," I warned him. I didn't like him taking only two of our guys with him, but I understood his need to keep April as safe as possible. I had that same urge running through my veins. Fuck, we all did.

He nodded once at me in understanding. "The rest of us have ten minutes to get a bag packed and be on the road once we're out of this room. It'll be a two-hour ride there, which means a four-hour round trip. I want everyone on their Ps and Qs. My goal is to find this son of a bitch and get answers out of him, but I'm not hopeful we'll be able to. But I at least want eyes on him. Clear?"

Grunts of affirmation rang around the room. Capone slammed his gavel on the table, and we all filed out of the chapel. The clubhouse was otherwise quiet—so quiet, in fact, that I could hear the crickets chirping outside. Malorie was still asleep in one of the downstairs rooms, thinking she was perfectly safe, and when I stepped into Capone's room with him, April was still curled up in bed, her lips softly parted in sleep.

I jerked to a halt when Capone slid his hand along the side of my neck and drew my lips to his for a soft, slow kiss. I sank into his embrace, my hands landing on his sides. My fingertips dug into his skin. "Do not let anything happen to them," he murmured against my lips, keeping his voice low so he wouldn't disturb April.

I shook my head. "Never," I quietly swore. "And you keep our boys safe out on that road."

He rested his forehead against mine, and we both shut our eyes for a moment, drinking in our connection. "I'll do my best," he promised.

I knew that was all I could ask of him.

———

I could hear Malorie moving around downstairs, and a quick text to Rider let me know he and River had eyes on her. Smokey was sitting in Capone's desk chair, vaping. I told him he could go outside and get his usual morning smoke, but he just shook his head, claiming while Capone and the rest of our men were gone, he wasn't leaving April's side.

I knew the change in his routine bothered him, which bothered me, but if he wanted to stay by her side, I wouldn't push him.

April was still asleep, and I'd already gotten a text from Capone to let me know they made it safely and he was going radio silent until they hit the road again.

I fucking hated radio silence. Because I had no idea what the fuck was going on when they weren't communicating. I wouldn't know if something happened until afterward. I wouldn't know if they needed help. None of that.

April moaned in her sleep, her face scrunching up. Tears suddenly slid down her cheeks. I quickly lurched to a sitting position, already reaching out to grab her in my arms when she screamed. It was loud, piercing my eardrums, and full of anguish and pain. A chill raced down my spine at the sound.

That sound would haunt my dreams for the rest of my life.

Her eyes flew open as soon as soon as I grabbed her, and she sobbed, falling apart in my arms, her entire body shaking. Smokey was already crawling onto the mattress with us by the time I had her cradled on my lap, my arms bound tightly around her, squeezing her to me.

"Capone?" she cried, her hands twisting in my shirt as she searched the room. "Where's Capone?"

I gripped the back of her head, holding her to my chest. Smokey wrapped himself around both of us, squishing her between us. "He's on a run, darlin',"

I gently told her, somehow knowing it would only make things worse. But I wouldn't lie to her. *Couldn't* lie to her. Our man wasn't here.

"Get him home," she croaked, her crying only getting worse at the news. "He needs to be home. She—oh, God, she's going to have him killed!" she wailed.

My heart stopped in my chest. She'd had one of her dreams, and while we'd been hoping for one, I didn't want this kind. Not one where she was screaming for Capone and yelling about him getting killed.

I only prayed I could get in touch with him on time. That it hadn't already happened. That maybe we could change fate.

Smokey reached for April's phone and snatched it off the charger, knowing if Capone would answer anyone's call while he was radio silent, it would be April's. He promised her he would *always* answer if she called, and I knew that no matter what he might be in the middle of, he would.

Because for her—and only for her—we ran by a different set of codes.

Smokey put the phone on speaker, and I waited with bated breath, gently rocking our woman as the phone rang. If he didn't answer, there was a chance she'd fucking lose it. Hell, I might, too. "April? What's going on, baby girl?" Capone asked, his voice quiet.

She sobbed, and Capone growled. I imagined that sound had his soul raging. If I heard her crying and wasn't near her, I'd probably lose my shit. "April, talk to me."

"Come home," she pleaded.

"Baby—"

"You *have* to come home," she cried. "Please, Capone. She's—you're going into a trap."

I was pretty sure if I had eaten breakfast, I would've thrown it up. Not much bothered me anymore, but the thought of Capone and our boys going into a fucking trap—getting themselves hurt or killed—sliced through my gut like someone had stabbed me.

"Hawke," Capone quietly snapped, "pull out. Now," he ordered. "April called."

That was all Hawke needed to hear to know they were going into something bad. Something dangerous.

Something they might not walk out of alive from.

I heard Hawke quietly giving orders to Brewer. A moment later, Capone came back on the line. "Tell me about the dream, baby girl. That's what you had, right?"

"Yeah." She sniffled, her tears thankfully slowing now that Capone was leaving—taking her nightmare seriously. "There was a phone call. She told someone you were coming. You walked into a room at an abandoned motel and —" Her words cut off as she sobbed, her shoulders shaking.

"Fuck," Capone swore, and that was all I needed to hear to know that was exactly where he was at. A fucking motel. I could probably place money on it that it would be the exact same one in her fucking dream.

It chilled the blood in my veins. So many people thought of her dreams as a gift, and when they protected our men, they were. But I knew they were also a curse. Because even if we managed to stop what happened in time, she still had to live with that fucking nightmare playing on repeat in her head.

I dreaded the day she woke up too late to warn anyone of what could happen. That guilt would eat her alive inside, and I knew nothing any of us did would ease the pain she would inevitably live with for the rest of her life.

"Easy, darlin'," I soothed, burying my face in her hair. "He's going to be okay."

Fuck, he *had* to be.

"Keep talking," Smokey urged, his hand running over her hair.

"Someone was waiting behind the door," she whispered. "I saw him rush out with a knife. His face was covered with a mask. And then, I woke up."

Smokey was pale. Fuck, I was sure I didn't look much better. If I'd dreamed what she had, I'd have been drowning myself in a liquor bottle.

Because Capone wouldn't have answered the phone for me.

I was more thankful than ever for April at that moment. Because losing Capone, Hawke, or Brewer would kill me.

"I'm coming home, baby girl, you hear me? I'm getting on my bike now," he promised her. "I'll see you when I get home. Let the guys take care of you."

"I love you," she whispered, her voice cracking. There was so much pain in those three words that I shuddered.

"I love you, too," he promised.

———

April was silent and withdrawn for the two hours it took our men to get back to the clubhouse. Smokey and I could barely get her to drink water to get her hydrated. Food was off the table; she couldn't stomach it. Just the smell had her gagging, so River quickly took that back downstairs.

Rider and River were deeply concerned, but they didn't dare let Malorie out of their sights after April's dream. We all knew the tendency those dreams had of coming true. Capone, who we all felt was nearly invincible, could have died today had April not had that dream. And if he hadn't answered her call like he promised he always would...

My temples pounded with an oncoming migraine at the mere thought of living in a world where Capone didn't exist. Something in me threatened to wither and die at the mere idea.

A world without Capone was miserable and bleak.

The sound of bikes roaring onto the lot had April jumping from my lap. She stumbled, and I barely managed to steady her before she was rushing down the stairs in nothing but one of Capone's t-shirts with no fucking panties, but Smokey nor I said a damn word.

She needed him. If Malorie got an eye full of April's cunt, then she shouldn't have been looking.

We hurried down the stairs after her, our boots pounding on the wood, and as soon as Capone walked through the clubhouse doors, April launched herself into his arms. He stumbled back into Hawke and Brewer, his hands grasping her thighs, his fingertips digging into her soft flesh. Hawke and Brewer quickly steadied them before they ran their hands over April's back and hair, doing their best to ease her worries as she cried into his Capone's neck and clung to him, her nails digging into the back of his neck hard enough to draw blood.

Capone cupped her cheek and forced her head up. He rested their foreheads together, and my heart broke as I watched her lips tremble. "I'm here, baby girl," Capone soothed. "I'm okay, and I'm home," he promised.

# CHAPTER 17

*Smokey*

Seeing April so distraught tore at my fucking insides. Left me feeling raw and splayed open. When what was bothering her was something I couldn't protect her from—like her mind—it made me feel crazy. Like I was out of control. It sent me back into the dark place I'd fought like hell to get out of. To *stay* out of.

Capone settled into a chair at one of the tables, his hands running over her hair and back as he let her cry it out. She'd saved his life today. There was no doubt about that. But the things she must have seen in her dream had to have been horrifying. I'd already heard most of it, but I knew it was nothing compared to essentially living through it like she had.

For a split moment, she'd lived in a world where Capone no longer existed. Where she had no idea if Hawke and Brewer were still alive. How she wasn't throwing up, I had no idea. Because even catching a glimpse of that kind of vivid nightmare would have me spewing everything I had inside of me.

Tank suddenly gripped the back of my neck, and I blinked before turning my head to look at him. He was crouched in front of me. Fuck, when the hell had I even sat down? Had I really been that out of it?

"You here with me, boy?" Tank rumbled, his concerned eyes running over my face. "You spaced out." His thumb stroked over my neck, and I shivered, focusing on his touch to ground myself.

April was no longer crying and was now swiping at her cheeks. She'd been transferred to Hawke's lap, and he and Brewer were softly talking to her. Christ, I'd been out of it a good minute. No wonder Tank looked so concerned.

"You know we'd never let anything happen to him, don't you, doll?" Hawke gently asked April, drawing my eyes to him.

"Daddy," her chin wobbled, "my dream—"

"Okay," Brewer said softly, his fingers combing through her long, dark hair. His eyes were tender as he gazed at her, his hand never stopping its soothing stroking over her hair. "Alright, sweetheart. Deep breaths, you hear me? You've got to tell us what you saw."

"Baby boy," Tank rumbled, drawing my eyes back to him, "light up, you hear me? Otherwise, you're not going to make it through this."

"I'm fine," I mumbled. But I still reached into the pocket of my cut and grabbed the long, slim container that held my rolled blunt.

"No, you're not," Tank retorted, not letting me downplay how I was feeling. "When she has these dreams, you're never fucking okay, Smokey. And I get it. We all get it. Which is why I'm telling you to smoke. You need to calm down, and honestly, our girl needs it, too."

I looked up when a shadow loomed over me, my hand in my pocket, trying to fish out my lighter. Hawke was holding April in his arms, and his intentions were clear. He was deciding to help both of us; he was going to give her to me to hold. She would be held and get to smoke, and I would get to feel like I was keeping her safe while I relaxed as well.

I quickly pulled my lighter out, lit up, and then patted my lap. Hawke gently set April on my legs, and I placed the blunt between her lips. Her eyes were red and bloodshot, still glassy with unshed tears. My heart splintered, and my fingers spasmed with the urge to do something—anything—to get rid of the uncontrolled sensations thrumming through me.

I couldn't do a goddamn thing to help her.

I pressed my lips to the top of her head. "You saved him, baby," I quietly told her.

She sniffled and slowly blew smoke from her lungs, but I could tell my words helped her. That—those three words—were what she needed to hear.

Capone dragged a chair closer and slid his hand over her thigh, and his fingertips brushed my thigh as well, comforting both of us. Our eyes met for a moment, and he nodded once at me before focusing on our woman. "Talk to me, baby girl. Tell me your dream. Every bit of it you can recall."

She drew in a deep breath. I grabbed one of her hands in mine, and Capone took the other with his free hand, both of us working together to keep her grounded. Tank settled his hand on my shoulder, standing over all three of us, his massive body casting a shadow over the three of us.

"Malorie made a phone call from behind the club-house after she told Tank she needed air," she said quietly. I placed the blunt between her lips, forcing her to take a drag before she continued. Once she blew out the smoke, she rasped, "I could only hear her side of the conversation, but she was telling someone your entire plan. Calling them baby and saying they were falling right into his trap. I don't know who *he* is."

Capone brushed his thumb over the back of her hand. "You're doing so good, baby girl," he praised. She was. She was being so fucking brave for reliving that horrible dream. For reliving what could have come true had she not woken up in time to warn Capone.

I took another hit from the blunt before forcing her to as well. Capone shot me a thankful look, which eased some of my discomfort that the weed couldn't melt away on its own. "My dream suddenly flashed to you. You were easing along a motel wall. The place was a dingy yellow with peeling, dark green doors, and the lot had weeds growing in the cracks of the asphalt." Capone's face tightened, and that was all the confirmation I needed to know that was the exact place he'd just been at.

I swallowed vomit.

"Hawke and Brewer—I don't know where they were. You were alone. I think you heard something. I was screaming at you to stop, but you couldn't hear me." Her breath hitched, and a tear ran down her cheek. Capone tightened his hand on her thigh just as I squeezed her hand. "You opened the door and stepped inside the room with your gun drawn, but it didn't matter."

*Fuck.* My leg began to bounce. Rider moved closer and clamped his hand on my knee, his fingertips biting into my flesh. It soothed me a little, the pain giving me something else to focus on besides the turmoil raging inside of me.

"They hit you with the door, surprising you, and you stumbled. Then, someone wearing a mask rushed out from behind the door with a knife." Tears leaked down her cheeks, but she wasn't panicking this time, which meant the weed was doing its job. "I don't know what happened after that. I woke up."

Everyone was on edge after hearing what she had to say, and it made me sick to my stomach. We all could have lost Capone today. Fuck, we could've lost Hawke and Brewer, too, and it made me feel violently ill. My hands shook. I sucked in a ragged breath, squeezing my eyes shut.

I felt useless. Twisted inside out. I could have lost three men that I desperately needed in my life.

Capone quickly grabbed April, tucking her head into the curve of his neck, and then Tank was yanking me up from my chair and holding me tight in his arms. "Breathe," he quietly ordered. He cradled the back of my head, massaging my scalp. "Breathe, boy."

I drew in a shaky breath, my chest fucking hurting. Someone took my blunt from my fingers, and I curled my hands into Tank's shirt, using him to ground myself. I was panicking; I knew that. Unfortunately, these fucking attacks just had to run their course. My breathing was ragged, and every breath fucking *hurt*.

My body trembled, my teeth chattering. Tears streaked down my cheeks. For what felt like forever, I thought I was fucking dying.

"Fuck," I croaked once my breathing had regulated and I didn't feel like someone was stabbing my lungs with a fucking knife. But now I was exhausted, my mind sluggish and my body tired. My eyelids drooped a little, and my body felt weak.

Tank buried his face in my hair, holding me even tighter, somehow knowing I needed his physical support as much as I did his emotional. "They're safe, Smokey," he promised. He pressed a kiss to the top of my head. "They're fucking safe."

*Tell that to my nightmares tonight.*

# CHAPTER 18

*Rider*

"Is April with River?" I asked as Capone stepped down the stairs, his boots thumping on the hardwood flooring. Tank followed in behind him with Smokey at his side, Tank's hand firmly clasped around the back of Smokey's neck. Smokey had spiraled, having a panic attack for the first time in months. I'd wanted to comfort him, but I wouldn't leave Malorie. If what April dreamed was true, which normally was, then Malorie was not only shady and two-faced, but she had a cell phone that she was using.

And I wasn't risking her getting in contact with someone. Not on my fucking watch. Not again.

We could've lost Capone, Hawke, and Brewer today, and that shit settled in my gut about as well as battery acid would.

"Yeah," Capone grunted. "Soon as he got upstairs, I told him to keep her occupied."

I snorted. "That shouldn't be too hard. Our woman is a slut for cock."

Brewer chuckled from his position in the corner. Hawke was next to him. Both of them were standing with their arms crossed over their chests, but their shoulders were pressed together. I would've loved to be over there with them, sharing in that quiet intimacy, but I was the torturer. I had the patience the rest of my men lacked, especially Capone. He was the most impatient mother fucker out of all of us.

I slid my fingers into Smokey's hair when he neared me and brought our foreheads together. Tank drew to a stop next to him, his hand still around the back of Smokey's neck. Smokey blew out a soft breath, the smell of weed infiltrating my nostrils before he pressed his lips to mine in a soft kiss. I deepened it for a moment, snickering when Malorie scoffed in disgust from the chair I had her tied to. It was the first sound she'd made since I'd dragged her into the basement while Tank, Capone, and Smokey were upstairs.

"You good, baby?" I asked him, opening my eyes so I could search his. They seemed a little lost, which made my soul roar in rage. But I knew we'd eventually bring him back to us.

He nodded. "Tank's got me."

I pressed a kiss to the corner of his lips, and he sighed, his body relaxing. "We've all got you, you hear me? Don't ever lose sight of that." I kissed the other corner of his lips.

He nodded. "I won't. Promise."

"Good boy," I murmured before stepping back and dropping my hand. Tank ran his fingers through my brightly colored hair before leading Smokey over to Hawke and Brewer. Hawke wrapped Smokey up in his arms and forced him to lean back against him.

Hawke was such a Daddy. But that title was just for April to use, which was fine with me. Our woman deserved everything in the world, and if we could give it to her, we would without hesitation. Besides, if *anyone* was Smokey's Daddy, it was Tank.

I shrugged off my cut, passing it off to Capone. He folded it over his arm, nodding once at me to get started. I then turned to face the bitch in front of me, pulling my knife from its holster on my belt. She eyed it but didn't say anything.

That was alright though. She'd be singing by the time I got done with her. Probably wouldn't even take much.

"Every time you tell me something I don't care to hear, I'll make you bleed," I warned her. "And I have more patience than any of the other men in this room." I crouched in front of her, resting my elbows on my knees. "Did you know I once tortured a man and managed to keep him alive while doing it for forty-eight hours?" A cold smirk tilted my lips. "He bled quite a bit. Not much left in him by the time I got done."

Her jaw tightening was the only response I got. I hummed and licked the edge of my blade, letting blood well up on my tongue before I licked my lips, smearing the blood there. Her pupils got a little wider in horror. I heard Capone quietly moan, and I grinned, blood no doubt staining my teeth. I turned to him and winked before focusing back on my prey.

"First question, Malorie. Let's see if you try to call my bluff, hm? Who sent you?"

"None of your fucking business," she growled.

I pursed my lips and nodded my head before I stood. Reaching forward, I cut her shirt open, straight down the middle, before I cut an X into her chest. She screamed through gritted teeth, sweat running in rivulets from her forehead and temples. I stepped back from her, eyeing my handiwork. It could've been a little straighter. I needed to brush up on my knife skills.

I locked my eyes back on her pain-filled ones. "Now, Malorie, let's try again, yes? Who sent you?"

"I'm not telling you shit. You'll just kill me anyway."

I snickered. "Yeah, I will, but it's up to you whether you die slowly and painfully or quickly with minimal trouble." Then, I stepped forward and cut a plus sign through the cross, making a sort-of fucked up looking asterisk. This time, she couldn't keep her jaw locked and screamed nice and loud, tears running down her cheeks.

A manic grin tilted my lips.

"Who sent you?" I asked again.

"My boyfriend," she hissed, blood running down her chest and stomach, staining her jeans. "Angel Lockwood. He's the president of the Burning Demons."

I kept my knife to myself, as promised. I was at least a man of my fucking word. That could be trusted, if nothing else about me could be.

I tapped my bloody knife against my other palm. "What does he want with this club?"

She shook her head. "I won't—"

I sighed. "You won't tell me?" I asked, cutting her off. I nodded my head. "Cool."

"Wait—wait!" she screamed. "Rider, please—" I grunted in disgust. The only woman I wanted to beg me was upstairs, more than likely getting slowly fucked by our sweet boy, River. The sound of her begging me was *wrong*, and I made the pain hurt just a little more than I normally would to stop my skin from crawling.

She screamed as I cut the beginnings of an R into her stomach, being careful not to go too deep. She sobbed, her belly shaking as she did so, ruining my artwork. Didn't matter. I finished the R and then stepped back. Blood dripped from the knife onto my boots, so I wiped it off on my jeans. My hands were an absolute mess, but it was nothing a good shower wouldn't get rid of.

"Let's try again." I arched a brow at her. I wasn't playing fucking games. "What does he want with this club?"

"You killed his brother for what he did to April," she sobbed, bleeding all over the place. "He wants to wipe your club out and make April pay."

Rage pulsed through me like a hot, live wire, but I contained it. Somehow, we all fucking did. It was a goddamn miracle. I even heard Smokey snarl something quietly, but Hawke gently shushed him.

"Is that why he beat you?" I demanded to know. "Because we took April in for the same thing?" Everything was beginning to add up nicely, and fuck, it made my stomach turn.

Our woman was in danger.

Malorie sobbed, nodding her head. "Yes," she cried. "I let him. Tony was mine, too," she cried. "And you fuckers ripped him from me. This was supposed to be the way we infiltrated your club."

So, not only was April's boyfriend a sadistic abuser, but he'd also been a fucking cheater. If I could, I'd bring him back from the dead just to kill him all over again. Because April hadn't deserved any of the shit he'd done to her. She was too pure for a world this cruel.

I shook my head, a heartless laugh spilling past my lips. Malorie's body quaked with fear. "You and your boyfriend are dumb mother fuckers," I told her. "And it's your fucking downfall."

Then, I plunged the knife through her neck and yanked it back out, blood spewing everywhere, coating the front of my body before I could step back out of the way.

Her face was forever frozen in a mask of pain and horror, and I watched as the life slowly left her eyes and she choked on her own blood. Capone slid his arms around me from behind, resting his chin on my shoulder.

"Good job," he whispered in my ear.

A tremble ran through my body at his softly spoken praise.

# CHAPTER 19

*Brewer*

I was sweating by the time the basement was cleaned up. All I wanted was a shower and to fall into bed before we got up stupid early for church in the morning. No doubt Capone would have a plan by morning time. And he would want to move on it quickly, especially since he'd managed to find Malorie's phone hidden outside, buried beneath some leaves by the fence. If this guy tried calling Malorie, it wouldn't take him long to figure out that she was dead. And we wanted to be on the move before they came up with a plan of retaliation.

"Fucking hell," Hawke groaned as he rolled his shoulders. "I'm hopping in the shower and going to fucking bed. Tell April I said goodnight and I love her, yeah?" he asked as he headed to the stairs.

"Will do," I promised, looking at Rider.

Rider was a fucking mess. Not only was he just as sweaty as I was, but he was also covered in dried blood and smelled fucking horrible. The scent of blood was metallic, and it made my teeth tingle like I was biting and dragging them over a spoon.

It wasn't pleasant in the slightest.

"You ready to head up?" I asked Rider.

Rider nodded. "You joining me in the shower?"

I huskily laughed and stepped up to him. Curling my hand around the back of his neck, I dragged him closer to me until our bodies were perfectly aligned. His dick was already hard, and I groaned at the sensation of his length against mine. It felt blissfully good—even through the layers of clothes separating us.

"Yeah, babe. I'll join you in the shower. Our woman could probably use a bit of cleaning up as well." Especially since she'd been upstairs with River for *hours*. She probably looked like a cum dumpster. I licked my lips at the sinful image. *Fuuuuck.*

PROPERTY OF CHAOS KEEPERS MC   183

Rider grinned and tilted his head just the tiniest bit before kissing me. I moaned into his mouth, tightening my hold on him as he gripped my waist, his fingers digging into my sides. I slid my fingers into his purple hair and then yanked his head back, forcing our mouths apart before we got carried away down here. "Upstairs," I growled when his eyes met mine.

He smirked. "Yes, sir."

*Little shit.*

When I released him, he spun on his heel. And just for his little bit of sass, I smacked his ass.

Hard.

He yelped and turned to face me, narrowing his eyes at me. "Playing a dangerous game, Brewer."

I chuckled. His warnings did nothing but turn me on more. I loved it when Rider got a little rough. "Get a move on, Rider."

He winked at me before spinning back around and heading up the staircase. I climbed up behind him, flipping off the light switch as I went. The main part of the clubhouse was empty as we walked through it. No doubt, everyone was already passed out in bed to be bright-eyed for tomorrow. Lucky fucks.

When we made it upstairs to River's room, he was asleep in bed, his arm thrown over April's waist. She was awake though, reading a book on her phone. She looked up at us when we entered, pressing her finger to her lips.

As if we'd wake up that sweet boy. Fuck, River was precious. But he was also a light sleeper, so we had to be extra cautious that we wouldn't disturb him.

"Come on," Rider whispered, gently easing River's arm from around her. I helped her off the bed as she stared at Rider's blood-stained clothes before grimacing, her nose scrunching in disgust. Rider bit back a chuckle.

"He needs a shower," I told her once we were in the hallway and heading to Rider's room.

She made a noise in the back of her throat that had me snorting out a laugh. "No shit. She's dead then?"

"Very," I confirmed as I pushed open Rider's door. I let her step in first before following in behind her. Rider was close on our heels, and he quietly shut the door before heading straight for the bathroom, already tugging his bloody shirt over his head. There would be no helping that shirt; it had to go straight to a burn pit.

"Feel free to join," I told April.

After pressing a kiss to the side of her head, I followed Rider into his bathroom. He was shoving his jeans down his legs when I stepped in. "Can you start the shower?" he asked.

I didn't say anything, but I did start the shower for him, turning the dial so it was his preferred temperature. He quickly stepped in, and immediately, the water turned red as soon as it hit his body. He groaned, his shoulders slumping forward as the water beat down on his back, loosening his tense muscles.

"Fuck, I'm tired," he muttered.

I stripped out of my own clothes. "We all are," I reminded him. Grabbing my phone out of my jeans pocket, I shot a text to Smokey, asking him if he'd get rid of our bloody clothes for us. Once he confirmed he would, I grabbed them and tossed them into a garbage bag before setting them out in the hall.

When I turned back around, April was standing naked in the middle of the room, a small smile playing on her lips. Immediately, I gripped her waist, tugging her closer to me. A soft moan spilled from her parted lips when my hard shaft rubbed against her soft belly.

I looked down at her, brushing my thumbs over her smooth skin. "You joining us in the shower, baby?"

She nodded. "If the offer still stands." A teasing little smile tilted her lips.

I growled and nipped at her bottom lip. She sighed, her eyes fluttering shut for a split second. "Always fucking stands," I told her before spinning her to face the bathroom. "Now get in there. I think our man needs some stress relief after the shit he did tonight."

She walked into the bathroom without another word, her sweet ass jiggling with every step she took. Fuck, she was so damn beautiful. We told her she was all the time, but I didn't think she realized just how stunning she really was.

No other woman could *ever* compare to her. Couldn't even fucking hope to.

Once she stepped into the shower, I walked in after her, shutting the door behind me. Rider's shower was big and easily fit all three of us with space still to spare. Which was fucking perfect for what I had in mind.

"Turn around," I told Rider.

A cocky little grin pulled at his lips as he turned and planted his hands against the wall, wiggling his perky ass in my direction. He was such a fucking tease.

His purple hair was wet and hanging around his ears, badly in need of a haircut. But the water that dripped from his strands trailed in rivulets down his back, pooling in each dip of his spine before moving on. It was a slightly hypnotizing sight.

"April, get on your knees in front of him," I commanded as I squirted lube into my palm. Rider was always prepared—fucker kept a pump bottle of lube in his damn shower. And last time we'd had a quickie in his closet—he was getting dressed and I hadn't been able to resist him—he'd had lube stashed in there, too.

One thing about Rider, he was *never* going to be unprepared for sex.

April sinking to her knees in front of Rider was fucking mesmerizing. She was sexy while still looking so sweet and innocent. And fuck, she looked so damn eager to have his hard, leaking cock in her warm, wet mouth.

Our girl was always ready for us to use her however we wanted. I couldn't get enough of it.

"Good girl," I rumbled as I slicked up my cock. Rider moaned at the slick, wet sound. April was watching us, her lips slightly parted, her breaths coming just a tiny bit faster than normal as she waited for me to sink inside of him.

"You ready?" I asked Rider as I rubbed my wet cock along his taint and hole.

He groaned from deep within his chest and nodded. "God, yes, Brewer. Fuck, please—*shiiiit*," he moaned, his head falling forward as I began to push inside of him. I growled, my fingers digging into his hips as I sank deeper and deeper inside of him. He was so warm and tight and—*fuck*, I could not get enough of him.

"Now, April," I snarled through clenched teeth.

I watched through slitted eyes as she wrapped her hand around the base of Rider's cock before slowly swallowing him to the back of her throat, taking his entire length in her mouth like a seasoned pro. He whined, one of his hands falling from the wall to slide into her hair. He clenched a handful of her dark strands and began to thrust into her mouth, which meant he pushed back on me, too.

God, it felt so fucking good.

"Fuck, baby. That's it. You're both doing so well," I rasped. "So fucking beautiful together," I praised. Seeing April with any of our men was beautiful, but there was something about seeing Rider fall apart when he was normally so put together that was just breathtaking. He was our torturer. Probably the one who was the most fucked up out of all of us. Seeing him let go like this was... God, there were really no words.

April moaned around Rider's cock stuffing her mouth, and Rider whimpered, then gasped when she did something magical with her tongue. He shuddered, his breaths panting out of him.

"I'm not gonna last," he warned her. "April, my girl—"

I smacked my palm over his ass hard enough to make it hurt, and he shouted her name, coming down her throat. April closed her eyes, her expression blissed out as she swallowed every drop he fed her.

I took over once she popped him out of her mouth and chased my own release. Pressing my face to Rider's damp back, I gritted my teeth and moaned his name as I came inside of him, coating his hole in my cum.

When I pulled out of him, he helped April to her feet and then backed her up against the wall, kissing her while he slid his fingers between her legs. I watched, my hands cradling Rider's hips, as he circled her clit. Within seconds, she was coming undone, crying out his name, her eyes rolling back in her head.

I pressed my lips to Rider's throat. "You're both so perfect," I rasped.

Rider reached down and squeezed my hand that was holding his hip in response. Then, he pulled April close to him, holding her in his arms. "Help me get her bathed so she can get to bed," he rasped. "She's still got River's cum leaking out of her."

I chuckled and moved them under the spray of water. Rider held her close while I bathed her, and once she was out of the shower and drying off, I bathed Rider as well before sending him on his way with her.

By the time I stepped into the bedroom, both of them were passed out, wrapped in each other's arms. Unable to help myself, I snapped a picture on my phone before setting it as my background. Then, I dropped the towel from around my hips onto the hardwood floor and slid into bed behind April, wrapping my arm over them both.

"Brewer..." she mumbled, her words heavily slurred.

I pressed my lips to her damp hair. "Go back to sleep, baby."

She wiggled closer to me, her ass pressing against my cock, and a moment later, her light snores met my ears. I brushed my lips across her bare shoulder.

April meant the fucking world to all of us, and come tomorrow, I knew we'd be taking the last steps needed to ensure her safety one hundred percent.

*Come after us, and we'll toy with you.*

*Come after her, and we'll become your personal grim reapers.*

# CHAPTER 20

*Rider*

"Prez, I don't like this," I told Capone as I waited for April to come downstairs. Smokey was already outside in the truck with River, waiting on us to get our asses on the move. I shook my head, rolling my jaw around. "You need more hands."

"They're after April," Capone reminded me. I sighed, getting annoyed with him. "I need you and Smokey with her. Tank, Brewer, Hawke, and I can handle ourselves, boy. Remember that."

I gritted my teeth and ran my fingers through my purple strands. Turning to face him, I crossed my arms over my chest, arching my pierced brow. "If you get hurt, I'll finish the job for them," I swore. "That goes for *any* of you."

Capone wrapped his hand around my throat tight enough to restrict my airflow, and my dick hardened in my jeans. Christ, he did this shit to me so fucking effortlessly. "One, watch your tone with me." I smirked—couldn't fucking help it. My man knew I was a brat. He growled low in his throat. "Two, we will be *fine*. I give you my word. We've got a solid plan."

"Everything okay?"

Capone released me, but not before he squeezed his hand just a little bit tighter. I turned to face April, taking her bag from her. "Everything's good," I assured her. "You ready to go, my girl?"

Her cheeks flushed, just like they always did when I called her that. She loved the little names we had for her. "Yeah."

Capone drew her into his arms and pressed a kiss to her lips. She gripped his cut, her eyes closing. I knew she was just as worried as I was. She didn't like this either. "Do as they say, you hear me? I can't concentrate if I think you're unsafe."

She cupped his face in her delicate hands, and he shut his eyes for a moment, relishing in her touch. The tenderness he showed her would always warm a part of my soul. A man would be soft for the right person, and she was our person. "I will. I promise." A sweet smile tilted her lips. "I'm a good girl, remember?"

Capone and I both chuckled before he kissed her again, squeezing her ass. She moaned into his mouth, her lips parting beneath his. With a growl, he released her and then gripped a handful of my hair in his hand, yanking my head back to thrust his tongue into my mouth. I moaned, greedily sucking on it before he pulled back, his eyes dark and hazy with lust.

"Keep her safe," he growled.

I nodded once, tightening my jaw. "Always," I vowed.

———

April was asleep in the passenger seat when we got to the safe house, and River's head was on my shoulder, his eyes drooping. Probably didn't help that I was combing my fingers through his hair either. It was his biggest weakness and put him to sleep quickly every single time. But shit, touching him like this was soothing for me, too.

None of us wanted River in on the action. Capone had brought it up a couple of times, but we always shot it down. It wasn't that we didn't trust River. We were all just super protective of our boy, and no matter how much we trained him, none of us ever thought he was ready enough. He was our baby, and we just wanted to protect him as much as we protected April.

Thankfully, he didn't take it to heart. I was pretty sure he liked being babied.

"I'll carry her inside if you guys can get the bags," Smokey said quietly as he shut the truck off in front of the secluded cabin. We were staying at a state park about two hours away from home, and we'd booked under one of our fake IDs to keep the fuckers after April off our trail. The last thing we needed was trouble when we were trying to keep her safe.

"We've got it," I assured him as I pushed open the truck door. River quietly groaned and stretched, his shirt riding up to reveal just a sliver of tattooed skin before he slid out of the truck behind me. I let down the tailgate and grabbed the two small duffels—one that Smokey, River, and I were sharing and the other solely for April's things. She was picky about that kind of shit, so we let it be, even if we did prefer to travel with as little as possible. River grabbed the few bags of groceries we'd brought along with us.

Smokey was waiting by the door with a sleeping April cradled in his arms as we made our way up to the door of the cabin. I fished the key out of my pocket and unlocked it before opening it so he could carry her to bed.

"Unpack those groceries," I told River, nodding my head in the direction of the kitchen. "I'm going to get a shower, and then I'll start making dinner."

"Want me to fire up the grill?" he asked. "I can get the charcoal out of the back of the truck."

I tugged him close to me, and he let loose a low groan. He was just about as needy as our woman, and I couldn't get enough of it. I swiped my tongue over his lips, and he stepped closer, pressing his hard cock against my thigh. "No, baby boy. Just put away the groceries and relax. I'll have Smokey get the grill going."

Pressing a kiss to his lips, I released him. Smokey slipped out of the room we were sharing with April and quietly shut the door behind him. "Hey, can you get the grill going?" I asked him. "I'm going to hop in the shower."

"Kind of pointless to shower and then get try to cook on the grill, isn't it?" he asked, furrowing his brows.

I shrugged. "Being in the truck for so long has got me crawling out of my skin." I hated sitting still. Not to mention, being in confined quarters for so long left me feeling wrong. Like my skin didn't fit my body. A shower always helped sort me out. Like a cleanse, in a way.

He nodded in understanding. I traced my fingers over the back of his hand as I passed him. He turned his head, his eyes meeting mine, and the corner of his lips tilted up the tiniest bit. When I peeked in on April before heading into the other bathroom in the hallway to quickly shower, she was still asleep, curled up on her side, her arms hugging the pillow her head was resting on.

*Fuck*, she was beautiful. I could stare at her all day. Looking at her, I just wanted to lock her away in a tower somewhere where the rest of the world couldn't touch her and contaminate her happiness.

*We'll keep you safe, my girl. You've got my word.*

————

April hummed under her breath as she played in Smokey's hair, braiding and unbraiding parts of his hair to keep her fingers and mind occupied. I knew she was worried about our guys. Hell, I was, too. They were radio silent, and while I knew that was necessary for not only April's safety but theirs too, it didn't make it suck any less.

We couldn't even distract ourselves with sex. When April was worried like this, sex was off the table. She couldn't get in the mood. Sure, we could play with each other without her, but she needed our support. Fuck, we needed *each other*.

For two days now, we'd been sitting here pretending to watch TV, sleeping, cuddling, and trying to find things to occupy our minds like walks, swimming in the lake, and even the little museum in the state park. But the distractions never lasted long, not when our men were kind of MIA.

River was curled up in my arms, his head resting on my shoulder, blankly staring at the TV across the room above the fireplace but not really seeing it. Smokey and I were doing our best to hold him and

April together. Hell, getting River to eat was a fucking headache. He had no appetite. I couldn't blame him, but he still needed to eat in case something went down. I didn't think it would, but we always needed to remain on top of what was going on.

At any chance, shit could go sideways.

"I hate this," April suddenly spoke up, her hands stilling in Smokey's hair. Smokey leaned his head back, frowning at her. She blew out a harsh breath. "We can't get a single fucking update?"

I looked at her in surprise. She normally held herself together pretty well, but the stress was evidently taking its toll on her. I hated that I couldn't take it away from her so she could just be happy.

Smokey propped his head back on her thigh to look up at her a little easier. His fingers wound around her calves, and he squeezed, grounding her. She sighed, her head hanging forward, her hair a curtain around her beautiful face, blocking me from seeing her. "We're all worried, but we have to trust them. Capone and Tank know what they're doing, and those two men would never let Hawke and Brewer get hurt," he reminded her. "They've done much more dangerous things than this before, remember?"

The most dangerous op the club had ever done was infiltrating the sex-trafficking ring Smokey was found in. It was pure carnage, but everyone had come out unscathed. It was a near miss for most of us, but we'd managed.

I was hoping what our guys were walking into would be a walk in the park compared to that shit.

April blew out a soft breath, but before she could speak, Smokey's phone rang. He quickly grabbed it off the coffee table and swiped his thumb across the screen, raising it to his ear. "Talk to me." After a moment, he cut his eyes to me and nodded once, and I relaxed, a grin spreading across my face.

That nod was everything I needed to know. All of our men were okay.

"Let us know when you're back at the clubhouse, and we'll head back," Smokey told whoever called him. When he hung up the phone, he stood to his feet and lifted April, making her squeak in surprise. Her fingers dug into his shoulders. "That was Tank. It's done, and our men are safe and unscathed."

"Oh, fuck yes," River groaned. Then, he slid onto my lap and wrapped his arms around my neck. I palmed his ass, bringing him closer. Smokey and April settled onto the couch next to us, and Smokey softly kissed her.

"Ain't got time to fool around, boy," I growled, but I kissed River anyway. Both of us would be sporting blue balls, but fuck, the mini-celebration was worth it.

"Don't care," he rasped into my mouth as he ground his rapidly filling cock against mine.

I moaned low in my throat at the feel of his shaft against mine and guided his hips, controlling his movements as I licked into his mouth. April rocked lightly on Smokey's lap, more for the movement than actually getting off since I knew Smokey wasn't hard enough yet. It was rare he ever actually got hard. Her half-lidded eyes were locked on us as River and I moved fluidly together.

"Hot, aren't they?" Smokey rasped against the skin of her neck, his eyes on us, too. "Aren't they just fucking beautiful together?"

River moaned at Smokey's words, his fingers digging into my shoulders. My hips rolled with his. Christ, the man knew exactly how to wind us up.

The phone suddenly rang again, and Smokey leaned forward to grab it, putting it on speaker for all of us to hear now that we knew everything was okay. "We're all here," Smokey told him.

"Come home," Capone ordered. River shuddered at the sound of his voice.

"We're on the way," Smokey promised.

He hung up and set April on her feet. River dropped his forehead to mine, his breaths a little choppy. "Continue when we get home?"

I smirked and squeezed his hips. "If you're a good boy, I'll get you off in the truck on the way back."

He quickly scrambled off my lap and rushed to get our things together. Chuckling, I stood to my feet and then tugged April to me, pressing a kiss to her lips. She curved into me, and a tear ran down her cheek, relief flooding her body. I licked it up before pressing a kiss to her forehead. "Take a seat, my girl. We're hitting the road in just a few minutes."

She nodded and settled onto the couch. Smokey stepped up to me, and I wrapped him in my arms. "You did good," I whispered in his ear. He'd handled this so fucking well, and I was so damn proud of him. It wasn't easy for him to not know how everyone was, but he'd handled it like a fucking champ. No panic attacks. No stress-induced cleaning sprees. He'd been calm the entire time.

He didn't say anything—just squeezed my sides. But that was enough for me. I just needed him to know I was proud because Smokey needed that affirmation, even if he'd never ask for it.

# EPILOGUE

*River*

Capone stepped into my room, his eyes running over my body. I'd been working out a lot more lately, wanting to be included more with club business, though I knew the guys were still kinda against it. I was a patched member, yet the guys babied me. But I'd joined because I wanted to belong to something. And yes, I belonged to them—no argument there—but I wanted to be equal to them.

Capone made me a deal finally; if I worked out more, built up my stamina and my bulk, practiced with weapons daily, and learned hand-to-hand combat, he'd let me in. So, I had. And yesterday, I'd gone on my first small run with them. We'd left early in the morning before the light even broke the sky and didn't get back until dark.

It'd felt… freeing. I was finally equal to them. Could finally be useful, just as they were.

When we got back home, Capone had then fucked me into the mattress, telling me how proud he was of me. And Christ, my dick was plumping even now just *remembering* all his growled praises.

"Hey," I rasped as I tugged my shirt over my head. I nodded at the package he was holding under one arm. "What's that?"

"The guys and I agreed you should give April this," he said, holding the box out to me.

I took it from him with a small frown. "What is it?" They hadn't mentioned giving her anything that I was aware of.

He stuffed his hands in his pockets. "I ordered her a property cut." My wide eyes snapped up to his. That was huge. Sure, April had always been ours from the moment Tank said fuck Capone's orders and gave her a safe place to stay, to recover, but this was on an entirely different level. A property cut was forever. It cemented that she was our old lady. That she belonged *to the club*.

"She's going to fucking cry," I warned him. April wore her heart on her sleeve, despite all the hell she'd been through. She loved each of us deeply and passionately in different ways—in just the ways we all needed her to, honestly. And she did it so effortlessly, like loving seven different men in their own love languages was second nature for her.

She'd been made for us. There was no doubt about that in my mind. And we were created to love her. Cherish her. Protect her.

But this cut? Yeah, it was going to rip her wide open in the most beautiful way.

Capone sighed. "Yeah, well, I'm sure Hawke will be more than happy to cuddle her until she calms down."

I snickered. Tears were not Capone's thing unless they were from orgasms and sex. He did his best to tolerate them, and he never let her see that he hated it when she cried. But he was always more than happy to let someone else handle her when she was crying. And Hawke, as her Daddy, was the best man for that.

I personally thought she was beautiful when she cried, even if she was crying because something was ripping her apart inside. And Hawke did, too. Besides, he loved the cuddles he got to give her.

Never thought the whole Daddy kink thing would ever be hot to me, but seeing April with Hawke in their dynamic was both extremely sexy and beautiful at the same time.

I set the package down and shrugged my cut onto my shoulders. Capone slid his hands along my ribcage and tugged me against him before leaning down to claim my lips. I groaned into the kiss, my arms twining around his neck so my fingers could slip into his soft, dark hair.

"April is downstairs making breakfast. I'll take over cooking, and you can give her our gift," he told me, his voice a little deeper and gravelly. I could feel his erection against mine, and it took every ounce of my restraint to not coax him into the bed behind me.

"Okay." I nodded my head and stepped back, reaching down to adjust my cock. Capone smirked, pressed a kiss to my forehead, and silently left my room. I blew out a harsh breath.

*Fucking cock tease.*

———

April was frowning at Capone and saying something quietly to him when I walked downstairs. He just pressed a quick kiss to her lips to shut her up and nudged her out of the way so he could take over cutting vegetables. She huffed, but then she saw me and beamed. Capone smirked behind her back.

She was so easily distracted sometimes.

"Sleep well?" she asked, making her way to me, Capone's overbearing ass forgotten. He silently chuckled as she walked away. "I heard the run went great." She cupped my face in her hands and leaned up on her tiptoes to softly kiss me. I sighed, using my free hand to tug her closer to me. Fuck, her kisses were the best. "I'm proud of you."

I smiled at her, the words of praise meaning more from her than she would ever know. Then, I held out the small package to her. Her eyes widened in surprise, and her cheeks colored a pretty pink as she tentatively reached out and took the package from me. The guys moved a little closer, wanting to see her reaction. Capone continued chopping vegetables, watching her from afar.

"What's this?" she asked softly, looking up at me and away from the small, cardboard box.

"A gift." I cleared my throat and waved my hand around. "From all of us."

She licked her lips before slowly ripping open the package. Her lips trembled when she saw the leather nestled inside, and gingerly, she took it out, dropping the box to the floor. When she unfolded it to read the back, she sobbed, tears streaming down her cheeks.

I could see the front from where I was standing. She had an old lady patch, the patch for our club, and then smaller patches for our names.

"Here," I rasped, stepping forward. I gently took it from her and helped her put it on. It fit perfectly, and she looked hot as fuck in it in just a pair of tiny ass shorts and a crop top.

"I can't believe you guys did this," she blubbered, staring down at it and fingering the leather.

Hawke stepped forward and drew her into his arms. "You're ours, doll," he told her, pressing a kiss to the top of her head. "And now, every time you step outside of these clubhouse gates, the world will know, too. Because you'll be wearing that cut."

She clung to him as she cried her pretty heart out. Then, Hawke released her and cupped her face in his hands, pressing a kiss to the tip of her red nose. "We love you, doll. We love you so fucking much. I don't think you realize you have a small army of men who would die for you. Who love you so fucking much, that I'm not sure any of us could ever live without you."

"I love all of you, too," she croaked. And fuck, we knew she did. Just as we knew the capacity of her love could not be contained to three simple words.

He pressed a kiss to her forehead, and then I tugged her into my arms. Kissing her cheeks, I tasted the saltiness of her tears. "Do you know how beautiful you are when you cry?" I roughly asked her.

She giggled and sniffled, shaking her head. Smokey stepped forward and gently swiped some of her tears away. The others were keeping a wide birth. It was a bit amusing. They were so bad when it came to her tears. Tank was alright, but if he didn't have to deal with it, he was happy to allow someone else to.

"You're always beautiful, but when you're this happy that you cry," Smokey quietly told her, "you're almost too fucking stunning to look at."

She hugged him next, her tears slowing, and finally, everyone else stepped forward, Tank crushing all of us once he got his arms around us. And when Capone joined in, I almost couldn't breathe.

"Suffocating," Brewer choked out from beneath Tank's broad chest.

I snickered and then choked when Tank and Capone squeezed harder. But the lack of oxygen was worth hearing our woman laugh in the middle of all of us.

**Want to see how Capone and Tank met?**
*https://BookHip.com/KQSFWZM*

## ALSO BY T.O. SMITH

Want to stay up to date on new releases, preorders, sales, and freebies?

Join my newsletter and be one of the first to know!

https://www.tosmithbooks.com/newsletter

## ABOUT THE AUTHOR

T.O. Smith believes in one thing - a happily ever after.

Her books are fast-paced and dive straight into the romance and the action. She doesn't do extensively drawn-out plots. Normally, within the first chapter, she's got you - hook, line, and sinker.

As a writer of various different genres of romance, a reader is almost guaranteed to find some kind of romance novel they'll enjoy on her page.

T.O. Smith can be found on Facebook, Instagram, Twitter, and now even TikTok! She loves interacting with all of her readers, so follow her!

Made in the USA
Las Vegas, NV
08 July 2024

92010888R00132